Praise for *This Fa. ... ... Enough*

"It is not surprising that Lynn Sloan was a portrait photographer, nor that she has turned to fiction writing. Her bent is an exploration of the truths of the human heart, and this collection demonstrates **her remarkable gift** for it. Possessing hugely different personalities and backgrounds, the characters are compelling, even those with small roles in the stories. **Sloan is inventive and fearless** in the situations in which she places her protagonists, and the results are painful, sometimes funny, and always illuminating. In every story **her continual flashes of insight, so precisely rendered, remind us again and again how heartbreaking in all its complexities is the human dilemma.**" —Sharon Solwitz, author of *Once, in Lourdes: A Novel, Blood and Milk: Stories,* and *Bloody Mary: A Novel*

"…**intelligent, beautiful storytelling.** Lynn Sloan's stories exhibit a worldliness not often seen in fiction, focusing on characters who illuminate the complexities of modern life through brilliant allegory. She has a superb eye for detail and nuance…. **Sloan's world is one of poverty and wealth, art and the quotidian, love and remorse, and in these apparent paradoxes she offers fascinating insights to the human soul.** What a pleasure it is to read…"—**Joe Ponepinto,** author of *Mr. Neutron*

"**Sloan's characters are rendered with sensitive and realistic detail throughout.** —*Kirkus Reviews*

"The stories in Sloan's collection are tragedies that **nearly break your**

heart, or often do . . . Though the underlying theme seem to be the same across stories, Sloan does a superb job of diversifying her characters and setting each scene on a new and fresh stage. . . . Every one of Sloan's characters is a monument to "what if" and "if only" . . .[and] remind us to . . . live fully in what you have, and to cherish everything without the "if.""—*Centered on Books*

"…engaging…. Reflecting Sloan's acute attention to humanity, her characters are varied and have depths that make them individuals I can care about…. The book leaves a flavor that lingers—not sweetness, but the mineral clarity of a deep well. It's a satisfying swig of human longing and learning."—*Story Circle Book Reviews*

". . . exceptional stories by a talented writer who understands that emotions are sometimes indefinable and conflicting, that facing adversity can require more than just courage, and that human feeling is complex and intricate. . .. a layered exploration of both human weakness and strength. . ..
—*Windy City Reviews*

Selected Praise for Lynn Sloan's *Principles of Navigation*

" . . . **a tender, thoughtful story** of a couple whose once happy marriage dissolves amidst the stress of infertility and infidelity—and unmet expectations. . . . quietly compelling. It is by no means a heart-pounding page-turner, but it is a page-turner nonetheless, **a subtle story that gnaws and needles long after the cover is closed.**"—*Chicago Book Review*

"… moving and vivid…. **unforgettable.**"
—**Sharon Darrow**, author of *The Painters of Lexieville* and *Trash*

" . . . fascinating and gripping."—*Centered on Books*

"[A]n **absorbing, poignant** novel that artfully distills the many ways in which love can fail us — yet also take us by surprise when we need it most."
—**Katherine Shonk**, author of *Happy Now?* and *The Red Passport*

" . . . an annunciation, a miracle, . . . this novel of generation, of stasis, and of transformation."—*Newcity*

"I wanted to turn the page—no, **I needed to turn the page.** The payoff at the end made me glad that I did."— *The Collagist*

" . . . this is a book which reeled me in slowly. . . . Any writer who can keep me thinking of their characters even after I have finished reading their story, is an author I can **highly recommend**. If you love literary fiction, **do yourself a favor and pick up a copy of** *Principles of Navigation* – I promise **you won't be disappointed.**"—*Caribou's Mom*

"Beneath their outwardly conventional surfaces, both wife and husband reckon with realities darker and deeper and wilder than they had grown up to expect. **For its psychological acuity and for its narrative grace,** *Principles of Navigation* **is at once deeply satisfying and unsettling.**"
—**Richard Hawley,** author of *The Headmaster's Papers, The Headmaster's Wife,* and *The Other World.*

" . . . a hauntingly beautiful tale . . . "—*Booksie's Blog*

Sloan pushes back against stereotypes of gender and familial life, making a claim to **a new and urgent sense of the domestic.**" —*Necessary Fiction*

"Select this for your book club and enjoy discussing the unexpected twists and turns that lead to the evolving image of an unconventional family."
—*Hungry for Good Books?*

This Far Isn't Far Enough

Stories

Lynn Sloan

Fomite

Burlington, VT

"Nature Rules" first appeared in *Shenandoah*; "Grow Animals" in *Ploughshares*; "Lost and Found" in *Tahoma Literary Review*; "Ollie's Back" in *American Fiction Volume 13;* "Safe" in *The Briar Cliff Review*; "Bird" in *Connecticut Review*; "The Gold Spoon" in *The Worcester Review*; "Sunshine Every Day" in *Inkwell*; "Call Back" in *Nimrod*; "A Little 1-2-3" in *Thin Air*; "The Collaborator" in *American Literary Review*; "A Paris Story" in *The Literary Review*; "Near Miss" in *Hawai'i Review*; "The Sweet Collapse of the Feeble" in *Puerto del Sol.*

ISBN-13: 978-1-944388-29-4
Library of Congress Control Number: 2017947982

Fomite
58 Peru Street
Burlington, VT 05401
www.fomitepress.com

For Jeff,
again and always

Table of Contents

Ollie's Back

@ollies_back It's eatin' time. Lowcountry Cookin'.
Dipped oysters, quail&more. Respond for time&place.

OLLIE PEERED FROM HIS KITCHEN, where Sol and Angel stirred and sliced, into his living room, still unable to believe that his third-floor ghetto apartment had morphed into what Simone called a pop-up restaurant. Her idea, her money, and Ollie's chance to climb out of the hole he'd fallen into. Angel had painted ninja skateboarders busting through the long cracked wall, and Ollie had bought mismatched tables and chairs from the Goodwill and spray-painted them black. The place rocked, maybe. What Ollie knew about cool came from Donnie. Cool, or pathetic? Shiny flatware, water glasses to be filled, vases with purple calla lilies. Calla lilies. Who was Ollie fooling?

At the wholesale florist, he'd heard Donnie whisper *the purple* even though he hadn't heard Donnie's actual voice in four years. At Dabney & Oliver's, the place the two of them had built from nothing into the best food restaurant in Providence and all of Rhode Island, Donnie ran the front of the house and Ollie ran the back. (Dabney was Donnie's I'm-not-Portuguese nom de restaurant.) Donnie knew how to pick flowers. He had style. Donnie was the fucking king of style.

Ollie heard the deep fryer sizzle: Sol on the porch outside the kitchen's back door, starting the oysters. Steamed cowpea shoots, corndodgers, quail breast with cheesy grits, and preserved fig cobbler would follow Cousin Nettye's batter-dipped oysters for opening night. No choices, no substitutions, don't tell me about your food allergies. BYOB. He checked his cell phone. Time to light the candles. He adjusted a calla lily.

Sweet, stuttering boy, take it easy. Ollie pressed the heels of his palms together as if that might drive out that voice. He did not want Donnie in his head, not tonight, not ever.

His phone buzzed: Simone. "Look out the window."

Below, a crowd blocked the sidewalk and the steps. The dry cleaner was closed, praise the Lord, and the neighbors wouldn't complain—Ollie had fed most of them trial runs of tonight's menu—but if the cops took an interest, opening night would be closing night.

"Where . . . you?" Anxiety brought Ollie's stutter on bad.

"Burgershake," Simone's name for the dive on the corner.

"How'm I . . . supposed . . . How'm . . . I going . . . to handle?" Dealing with diners had been Donnie's job. Ollie touched his collarbone where the crucifix Donnie had given him used to rest.

Simone sighed. "I'll come up."

Simone was supposed to be his silent partner. With her shoe-polish black hair and her bulldog jaw, she looked fierce. Back in the day when she was a Friday night Table Two regular at D&O's, Donnie had said she was a clean-hands lawyer, even though it looked like she wore NFL shoulder pads under her expensive suits. Ollie didn't doubt she could control a crowd.

Grateful, Ollie turned toward the kitchen and shouted at the twins, *"De volada!"*

Minutes later, Simone appeared at the back door and sidestepped through the kitchen into the living room. "I'll buzz them in and get them seated."

Three months ago she'd showed up at Loni's Grill, the 24-hour dump where Ollie had landed after bouncing down the Zagat scale. "What happened to you?" she'd asked. He was so overjoyed to see someone from the good D&O days, he'd said, "Hard times," instead of, "What the hell do you think?"

When the cops thundered into D&O's kitchen, Ollie had cried out for Donnie, but in the hours and days that followed, he learned that Donnie had been dealing cocaine out of a storage locker by the harbor. That and all that it implied about Donnie having a secret life ate through Ollie, and he told the cops the truth. He knew nothing. *Can't be. Yes, partners . . . but Donnie . . . he handled . . . business side. Don't know . . . about . . . storage locker. Don't know. Don't know.* When they understood that Ollie was as stupid as he said he was, they let him go. At every place he'd gone after that, he'd failed, like Donnie had said he would. *You need me, sweet boy.*

A few nights later, Simone was waiting in her black Lexus at the end of his shift. "Get in."

She missed Dabney & Oliver's, best restaurant in Rhode Island, no, all of New England, hadn't had a decent meal since, yammered on about what Ollie could do with a good cut of lamb, his meat pies, the heavy Anglo food that had been D&O's specialty. Asked if he'd seen Donnie. Ollie shook his head. Let not thy tongue give voice to thy thoughts, as Pappy used to say. Donnie had led the way out of Monck's Corner up the Atlantic coast to this too-big, Yankee city. They were both eighteen and a pair of hicks. Ollie had trusted Donnie, had trusted everything to Donnie, who now was serving four to fifteen for Class 1 felony possession of cocaine. And D&O was history. Simone went on and on about how there was no decent place to eat within a hundred miles. By this time they were sitting in the square watching early-shift workers trudge toward the office towers. What kind of restaurant would he have if he could pick? She had some money to park. She missed hanging out at Dabney & Oliver's. She'd kind of like to own a restaurant, not that she knew the first thing. She kept circling back until he was tired and cold and wanted to go home. She asked what new angle he thought would succeed here in Providence, where the upscale options were limited to lobster and food that kept forever in a barrel.

He said, "Lowcountry," and here he was running a kitchen again, preparing twenty-six four-course meals out of his 7x10 foot kitchen with a four-burner stove, an electric deep fryer on the back porch, and the help of Sol and Angel, the twins from downstairs, while Simone ushered in groups of twos and fours and pointed to where they should sit. Ollie nudged aside Sol and lowered the flame under the grits.

When Simone popped in, "show time," grabbed a corndodger, and disappeared, Angel hurried out to open the wine bottles that most groups had brought with them. Ollie plated the oysters, and Sol helped Angel carry them out.

The week of rehearsals had paid off. A few snags, but okay. The sweat and hurry in the tight kitchen felt good—the sizzling, the steam, the heat, the back and forth with the boys. A few times he glanced up expecting to see Donnie smile at him from the dining room, then remembered the betrayal and pulled himself back by focusing on the one and only thing he could do well: abracadabra the raw harvest of fields, forests, and sea into food that pleased. By dessert, everyone was shoving bills into his apron pocket. Into the twins' too. The buzz almost lifted him off his feet. He was back. He was really back. He could do it on his own.

When the last of the diners had left, Simone reappeared from his bedroom, told him to leave the cleanup to the twins. Time to count. He carried in two shot glasses and brandy. She divided the cash, mostly hundreds, into stacks.

"Cash at . . . door. You are . . . good." He filled her glass, less for him, his hand shaking. In the kitchen he'd felt so sure, but now the lights were up and the cracks showed. Angel's painted ninjas looked like what you'd see in the alley. Why would people come twice to this dump?

"The yahoo with the Rolex couldn't believe I turned him away." Simone pushed her glass forward for a refill.

"How . . . many?"

"Turned away? Four parties of four. I said next time they'd come in first." She patted the stack of money. "2,700. Pure gold."

"And." He reached into his apron pocket for his tips.

Simone thumbed the bills like a pro. "A total of 3,940. Not bad for our first night."

Ollie teased out four hundreds to pay Sol and Angel, along with a couple extra twenties. "We're a . . . success?"

Simone clinked his glass. "Say it again."

Hiding his thankfulness and disbelief, he paid the twins and returned to see that Simone had unbuttoned the waistband of her suit skirt and the brandy level had dropped an inch. She was settling in, but he was exhausted and wanted her gone. He said, "You want, I'll pay Vin." Vin was their purveyor. "For next weekend, I'm thinking cheese straws, terrapin soup"— he never stumbled talking about menus or food—"Pee Dee chicken bog, chainey briar, and peach pie with my Aunt Ida's caramel sauce." Though he had doubted there would be a second weekend, he had planned a menu. "Terrapin, chainey briar won't come cheap, but Vin says . . . he can get."

"You're making this up, aren't you?" She laid her heavy paw on his, meaning she'd pay Vin, then pulled out some bills for Ollie's walking around money. Eighty/twenty partners. He was lucky to get twenty percent. After the cops closed D&O's and seized every asset they could lay their hands on, all Ollie had left was his reputation as the chef who'd eluded the law and let his partner take the rap. Donnie was beloved. Donnie could screw everyone and still persuade the angels on high that he was blameless. For her eighty percent Simone had fronted every dime from the Goodwill furniture to the rice shipped from Charleston, plus she covered Ollie's rent and all, and bought a used truck for him to run supplies. Vin wouldn't deliver in this shitty neighborhood.

"Pee Dee chicken bog?" she asked.

"Chicken and rice. Pee Dee's where it comes from."

"Chainey briar?" She reached for the brandy, which was empty.

"Vines, vine tips." He could smell the piney woods and taste the tang.

Simone nodded as if he'd sought her approval. "That's fine. Any more of this tucked away?" She tapped her glass against his.

"Nope." Eighty percent didn't give her the right to be over-the-top galling. "I'm tired, Simone." He wondered again where she lived. All he had was her office address, near the statehouse, and her cell number. He'd barely known her in the D&O days.

She inhaled a lungful. "I'll be by on Wednesday. We'll talk details about next weekend." She scooped the cash into her purse and stood, not bothering to button her skirt, and leaned over to kiss his shaved head. The touch of her lips made him think of eel.

"To a great partnership."

@ollies_back By demand. Fri/Sat nites. Drumfish. Duck. Grandma Orton's donuts w/bourbon sauce & more. Respond for tm&place.

Six weeks in, Ollie's Back was a success. No cop hassles—Simone must have paid them off—no neighbors' complaints—Ollie fed the building and half the block—and they had worked out their routine. Simone waved in each party, palmed their cash in her left hand, pointed with her right to a table, and Ollie pulled out the chairs. When the front room filled, he guided the next groups to his former bedroom. Turning his bedroom into another dining space had been Simone's idea: a bedroom he used six hours a day, or eighteen more seats and four grand more per weekend? His air mattress and one box of clothes hid behind a black curtain; everything else was in the basement. He needed no other home than Ollie's Back.

He signaled to Simone, Table Eight. No more. She let in the pair with the matching cowboy boots and shrugged at the disappointed who remained on the landing.

"Corkage?" Table Four called. "Here here." "Us too."

Angel dashed around with a corkscrew. Ollie angled toward the kitchen. Time to plate the duck breast.

A ham-faced guy he'd seen before grabbed his hand. "Great idea. Love this place." Across the room, Simone raised an approving eyebrow.

One beat later, a sinkhole opened inside Ollie. The guy was one of the big-tippers Donnie used to bring into the kitchen for a chef chat. If Ollie stammered too bad, Donnie would cover for him. Ollie touched his collarbone, wishing he could carve out all memory of those days.

"You . . . found us," he managed to get out. From the kitchen came the smell of butter going from golden to caramel. His tongue curled around the pearl of flavor, pulling him back. "If you want to eat . . ." He turned toward the kitchen.

"Bet you miss Dabney."

Ollie pretended not to hear.

❖

Sweet boy.

The first time Donnie called him that, he'd been so scared.

Monck's Corner Community College. He and Donnie had been held back after their culinary arts class. Chef Cecil something-or-other told them to scrub down the stainless steel tables again because Donnie had whispered during the demonstration. Aiming two fingers at Donnie, then Ollie, Chef Cecil Fat Ass retreated to his office on the other side of the glass wall as Donnie shot him the bird. Ollie, furious at Donnie for getting them in trouble, turned on the radio—gospel music wailed—then grabbed some rags and a spray bottle. He didn't want to get kicked out. This class was his ticket out of washing dishes at LuRain's Cafeteria.

Donnie's breath warmed the back of his neck. In the office, Chef Cecil was hunched over the phone.

Ollie placed his hands on the table, stiffening. "I've got to finish this and get to LuRain's."

"Sweet boy. This class is for shit." Donnie reached around Ollie and shoved aside the rags. "I've got a plan. You and me."

A plan. A thrill snaked down from his throat to his groin. A plan. It sounded like a song the way Donnie said it. Ollie pressed his hands onto the table to steady himself as he looked around at the dinged metal cabinets, the leaky fridges, the row of donated ranges missing knobs, trying to imagine the wide-open future that he'd prayed for, without any real hope. He wasn't smart, he stuttered, he had no money and no idea of how to get where he wanted to go. But Donnie Cardosa with the twisted smile and tight jeans, Donnie Cardosa, the coolest guy in class, had a plan, and that plan included him.

"Sweet boy, let's go."

In the living room, the ham-faced guy's laugh pierced the din. Ollie turned to the small plates spread out on the board over the sink, the staging area—returning dishes would go in tubs on the porch—where Sol had arranged the sliced duck diagonally over sprigs of cress. Heart knocking—would Donnie never be gone from his mind?—Ollie turned off the flame under the butter and drizzled peppadew sauce over the smoked duck, Sol following with sea salt flakes. The fragrance of sweet/sour layered over the scent of smoked and singed bird eased Ollie's dismay. Angel positioned the second staging board above the first, and they kept going. Forty-six of everything, which should be beyond the capabilities of this kitchen, but they were pulling it off, week after week. This Ollie could do. In a kitchen he could hang on and skate through whatever came his way.

Simone grinned from the door. "Smells good."

"We're coming through," Ollie said, snatching the bandana off Sol's head as the twins marched into the dining room, their arms bearing small plates. The back screen door slammed behind her.

After the first course, Angel hustled plates and Sol stayed by Ollie in the kitchen. Heat on, off, ladle, cut, scoop, slice, trim, arrange, dab drips in a close-quarter dance.

At the end of the night, the dishes washed and the kitchen cleaned, Sol and Angel took the extra food downstairs, and Ollie stared out his front window, too tired to eat his duck sandwich. Burgershake was dark. Inside the Lovely Coin Laundry, a couple of women leaned against the window. A police cruiser paused and kept going. This had been his view for the past four years. Donnie, who'd been with him everywhere, had never seen it. This apartment, this view belonged to Ollie alone.

A knock at the back door. Simone. "As promised." She held up a bottle of homebrew. "What are you doing in the dark?" She flipped the switch, sailed through the kitchen into the front room, sat opposite his uneaten sandwich, took a bite, and opened her purse. Inside was a wad of bills wrapped in a rubber band.

"Tonight we brought in just shy of five K—some bozos overpaid—plus whatever's in your pocket."

Hiding his annoyance—the sandwich, her attitude, her coming back at all—he retrieved the cash he'd tucked behind the fuse box.

"Bring some glasses," she called.

As she counted, he poured her homebrew. It smelled like *amarguinha*, that too-sweet Portuguese liqueur. He sipped. Almond coated his tongue. It was *amarguinha*, and it was Donnie's recipe, Donnie's one lousy recipe. A trail burned down his throat. What was Simone doing with this? Had Donnie given it to her before he went to prison? Why would he? And it had none of the sediment or cloudiness of five-year-old homebrew. Or had he given Simone the one recipe that he'd promised but never given to Ollie? She was only a fucking female diner.

"Altogether 6,350 bucks," she said. "Here's three for Sol and three for Angel, and more for you." She slid forward three stacks, her black eyes unblinking. She was waiting, he could tell, for him to ask about the *amarguinha*.

He concentrated, forming each syllable. "This morning Vin grumbled about payment."

"I'll take care of Vin." She eyed Ollie. "He asked about you."

He. She meant Donnie.

"He's concerned about you."

The pressure in his chest swelled to nearly unbearable. A heart attack? Sweet Jesus, not at thirty-four. He was skinny. He'd quit smoking. He turned to the window, sipping air, fighting the pain. Outside the Lovely Coin Laundry, the hooker with the pink wig leaned on a parking meter.

"Listen," Simone said. "I want what's best for both of you."

Inside his chest he felt crackling, like a slow-motion fist going through glass. "Tell him I'm . . . fine." What the hell was going on? "Let's stick to business. You and I . . . we . . . have been doing . . . fine."

She re-filled her glass. "We don't get a big allotment of friends in this life, Ollie."

"Oh fucking . . . please."

"Think twice before you burn them."

"Burn? Donnie burned me. Did he give a shit? Did he give a shit about what we had? Did he come to me and say . . .?" He shook his head, still unable to believe what Donnie had done. Donnie had abandoned him. "I could have gone . . . to . . . jail, and I didn't know a fucking thing. He's concerned? He . . . hung . . . me . . . out to dry. If they'd . . . I could have gone down too."

"Could have, would have, should have: Donnie feels the same." She gazed around the room, like some goddamn mama queen of the universe.

"The past is behind you. He's practically your brother. A brother, Ollie. You forgive a brother. Go see him."

Brother? Is that what Donnie had told her? Ollie stared past her at Angel's ninjas.

She pushed up from the table. "We'll talk about this later."

Later didn't come the next week. Ollie refused to think about Donnie. He planned meals. He worked out at the gym, where Sol sneaked him in. The weather turned hot. The electricity in his apartment couldn't handle AC, so Simone arranged permits for "family picnics" in different city parks each weekend. Friday and Saturday mornings Ollie set up the grill at dawn, left Sol to tend the hog or whatever—sometimes they ran an extension cord for the deep fryer, too—and returned around six o'clock with Angel, the prepared sides, and the dishes, flatware, everything they needed. Simone no longer came, a relief. She sent Rod, the guy who sent out the tweets, to string up lights, control the gate, help serve, and at the end of the evening settle with the twins. She controlled the money. Ollie saw her once a week, on Sunday mornings, when she came by with his cut and they'd talk about what had gone on. Rod was her eyes and ears.

She mentioned Donnie now and then, but she didn't push. As the summer went on, she dropped her Donnie talk altogether, content, he guessed, because business was good, very good, more than they could handle. Rod limited the crowd by texting the location an hour before to the first sixty who'd reserved spots. Twelve grand plus tips, sometimes sixteen per weekend. She said they needed a permanent space. Ollie'd been afraid to hope for this. A real restaurant. He'd get back most of what he'd lost. Most. A realtor friend of hers took them around to look at what was available.

@ollies_back Hog w/ all the trimmin's. Respond for tm&plc. #RIfoodies.

On the second Sunday in August, Ollie sat by his living room window working out his shrimp order for next weekend—fifteen years in the business and he was no better at math than he'd been in sixth grade—when Simone sashayed in with a bag of *malasadas* from Silva's, Donnie's old favorite. Ollie tensed but tried to hide it.

"Took some of these up to Donnie last week. 'Course they weren't hot like this by the time I got there." She plopped the grease-stained sack on his papers.

"Why are you on about this?"

She pushed aside his papers and sat. "He's up for a probation hearing at the end of the year."

So soon? Ollie ignored the pastry she shoved at him.

"They need to know that he has a job waiting."

"He has a job?" His stomach pitched. That's what this was about.

"I'll write the letter. You'll sign it."

"Ollie's Back isn't legal." As if she didn't know. "No license, no tax number, no payroll and all that shit." Like a jackass, he ticked off each point on his fingers.

"I nailed a lease on the place by the pier."

First she hits him low with Donnie; then she comes in high with the place he liked best, although he thought he'd hidden this fact. Then, like a goddamn prizefighter, she comes in low again by not even consulting him.

She smiled her got-ya-by-the-balls smile.

He touched the spot where his crucifix had been. "When do we begin?"

"Lease starts next week. Things go right, we open September 20. Maybe October 1." She reached for another pastry. "Aren't you happy?"

He re-filled her coffee cup. "Location's great. But that place . . . needs work." If she could sign the lease, she could sign the goddamn letter. "The rent?"

"Don't worry about it." She licked sugar from her fleshy lips.

"When are you going to . . . going to bring me in . . . on the business side?" He should have pushed earlier. He'd drifted, like always. And how much of the money she'd socked away was earmarked as his, if any?

"Don't worry."

He stopped himself from slant-eyeing the kosher saltbox in the kitchen where he kept his money. Salted away. Jackass. "I need to know more."

"Need? We're going to *need* more than Sol and Angel to get going."

"Why don't you sign the letter?" he said.

"I don't sign. Clean hands, remember?" She stood, waggling her hands, and nodded at his calculations. "How about dirty duck instead of shrimp?"

Dirty duck was Cajun, not Lowcountry. "Ooo-kay." Swallowing his fury he wrote on his notepad. "Dirty duck it is. And okra and tomatoes, collards to go with the duck, hog, as usual, and banana pudding." He tore out the page and handed it to her for Rod's Wednesday tweet.

From his window, he watched her drive away. This whole thing was a set-up for Donnie, right from the beginning. Ollie stood and kicked his chair. The night Simone had showed up at Loni's, the oh-so-surprised way she'd eyeballed him should have told him she'd come looking. If she'd told him upfront that Donnie was coming back, he would have stayed at Loni's. They knew that. But they expected him to be so shit-faced happy running his own house again that he'd cave. To make one hundred percent sure, Simone waited to push until they were at the get-serious real estate stage. They were a team. But why?

His head hurt from thinking. He paced from his front window to the kitchen. He had seen nothing between them back at D&O's. Not a gesture. No sign of special understanding. No wrinkle in the air between them.

He couldn't think. He needed to cook, needed to cook big. From his saltbox he pulled out 7,700 dollars. Plenty. He knocked on Sol and Angel's mother's doorbell. Angel opened, his mother behind him.

"I want to throw . . . a party, a blast-out . . . a big . . . dinner. Nothing to do . . . with business. Neighbors only. Tuesday night." Angel looked puzzled. "*Martes*. Right, two nights from now." Could he take over the back yard, set up the grill, tables, the works? Mom crossed her arms. Sol appeared. They were in.

"Spread the word. Free meal. Six o'clock."

Early the next morning, he took seven hundred bucks and drove into the country to buy produce and eggs from a truck farm he'd used back in the D&O days—he didn't need Vin telling Simone—and he bought a hog retail.

Shrimp and grits, keep it simple, hog, collards, blackberry pudding. No Rod tweet.

In the morning, after carting tables, chairs, dishes and flatware down to the yard, he sent Angel with cash to buy the shrimp. By mid-afternoon, as Ollie and Angel cooked the sides upstairs, the scent of roasting hog from Sol's grill floated through the windows. When Sol called up, "*Rapido*," Ollie stepped onto his back porch. The tiny, retired white couple from above the Lovely Coin Laundry stood by the serving table. He and Angel hustled the food downstairs as the hooker with the pink wig pushed open the gate. She paused, adjusting her gold halter-top while she winked at Ollie, her sly smile was just like Donnie's. That was it. Donnie had led Simone on, and she had fallen. Simone loved Donnie.

Familiar faces flooded in and Ollie hurried to the grill. As he checked the meat that Sol had sliced and sampled the sauce, his brain buzzed with this revelation. It had to be true. Donnie didn't love Simone, that was for sure, he couldn't. He was playing her, like he'd played Ollie.

The Korean guy from the car wash brought a beer-filled cooler and most everyone brought six-packs. Soon the yard was packed. Sol sliced, Ollie dished—not thinking, his nerves sparking, his brain a jumble—and Angel kept things moving. Salsa pulsed from a boom box on the stairs, where the teenagers had carried their food. Smoke, laughter, music. After a while it felt like the juke joints back home. And the folks kept coming. Someone brought out more folding chairs. Moving like he was trying to outrun a freight train, Ollie filled plates. "Bit more of them collards, if you please." "Just a dab of grits." "Not that fatty piece. Yeah, that's good." A blur of intent, eager, smiling faces.

A woman with a couple of toddlers in tow cut in front of Ollie and held out her emptied plate, shaking her head to his offer of more food. She was leaving. What should she do with her plate?

He'd forgotten dish tubs. *You don't think things through, sweet boy. That's why you need me.*

To the woman Ollie said, "Throw it in the dumpster."

She didn't understand. The plates, all of this stuff except the food, belonged to Simone. He grabbed a few fresh plates. "Here, take . . . these too."

The woman's eyes widened and she backed away, holding her dirty plate. Ollie considered tossing the plates he held over the fence—he would like the racket of plates breaking—but he put them down instead. Donnie was right. He hadn't thought through any of what came next.

"Listen up, you all," he shouted. "Listen, everyone." Someone dialed back the boom box and the crowd quieted. He worked out his words. "We're not washing dishes tonight. So take them and the flatware and throw everything in the dumper out there." He jerked his hand toward the alley. "No breaking . . . please. No . . . mess. I'm closing down. This is . . . farewell dinner." A murmur broke out and Sol raised his eyebrows in disbelief.

"So eat 'til there's nothing left but the burp," Ollie said.

Tomorrow he would pack his knives and head west. Vancouver Island maybe. Coastal. A continent away. In a day or two, Vin would call Simone to say that he hadn't heard from Ollie, and she'd send Rod to check. Sol and Angel would say, "*no comprende.*" Ollie grinned, imagining Simone telling Donnie.

Sol stepped close. "What the fuck you doing? We got something going here, you, me, Angel."

"The grill, fryer . . . what's upstairs, take . . . before Boss Lady comes . . . 'round. Start up something somewhere else."

"But why?"

"It's over. That's all."

In that shitty culinary classroom when Donnie kissed his neck, he had been electrified. Sure that he would die, he'd lifted his hands to turn and accept what was to come, but before he shifted his weight toward Donnie, he saw on the stainless steel table two skeleton hands, his own sweaty prints, and he watched the fingers narrow into lines and the palms shrink into smudges and then disappear. Now he was back.

Grow Animals

ON THE PLASTIC MONTHLY CALENDAR stuck to the refrigerator, Michelle hadn't bothered to write the dates in the little boxes. Monday was Monday, Tuesday was Tuesday. The dates didn't matter. Desmond's routine filled the days: school = red dots, occupational therapy = orange dots, water therapy = green dots, speech therapy = yellow and brown checked dots. The stickers formed a lively zigzag pattern when Michelle squinted, even though it was all routine. Her own few appointments were made when Desmond was in school, so these she didn't mark down. The point of the calendar was to teach her son about time. Desmond, at six, was not, and would never be, okay in the way that "okay" was generally thought of. The blue dots at the bottom of the Friday lineup she'd added three weeks ago, after her eHarmony meltdown, when Henry, her brother, had started coming over for dinner, "if you don't mind feeding me," pretending his visits weren't missions of mercy. She didn't know what was worse, that her younger, dweeb brother felt sorry for her, or that she felt grateful.

She took out plates for dinner. "Make way, buddy," she said to Desmond, behind her.

Working the joystick, he backed up his wheelchair so she could walk between the cupboard and dining room.

With the dining room table set, she sat on the kitchen stool opposite Desmond, uncurled his tight grip on the control wand of his chair and massaged his hand until it opened. She aligned her palm with his, lined up her long fingers with his small rigid ones, slowly threaded hers through his, until he grinned. Then she pulled away, her fingertips lingering on his until she lifted her hand, and waved—their old game, played since before words made any sense to him. She began again, her palm to his, her fingers with his, twisted them together, pulled apart.

He looked up at her, his jaw trembling. He was learning to talk and every word was an agony of effort.

"Mar . . . ee . . . Hen?"

Marry? She lowered her forehead to his, rolling her head from side to side, murmuring no. *Et tu, Desmond?* Henry had brainwashed her son when he babysat during her miserable eHarmony dates. Ever since, Desmond would ask about her getting married whenever Henry was due, or when any man crossed their path—the aging hippie with the grimy ponytail who lived across the hall, the grocery delivery guy, the gay receptionist at the rehab clinic they visited three times a week. Possibly Desmond's question was a cover for his real question: why didn't he have a dad? Sperm donor was not a concept he could understand, maybe never.

"You can't marry your brother, silly. And besides, you are my one and only."

"Love . . . Hen . . . ?"

"I do love Uncle Henry." She stood up to peer in the oven at the lasagna, evading Desmond's watery brown eyes. "And Poppa and Nona," whom she avoided as much as possible because of how jittery they became around Desmond. "And Maybelline," their snarling, blind Airedale bitch.

The doorbell rang, two long and one short. Henry. Desmond squealed, spun his wheelchair around, and zoomed down the hallway toward the front door.

"Slow down." He couldn't turn the knobs.

She poured her first glass of wine, enjoying the lovely gurgling sound. She'd been waiting for this moment, but she refused to drink alone. Before Desmond, BD: Rules about small stuff were the mark of boring people. AD: Establishing and maintaining rules were essential. And besides, Desmond slept with a monitor. She couldn't take a chance.

The wine, tart and chill on the tip of her tongue, curling along the back, sliding down her throat, eased the tightness she never noticed until it loosened. She loved this moment that seemed to promise goodness ahead. True, on any given Friday night BD, she wouldn't be eating fattening lasagna and sipping no-buzz white wine. She'd be slamming through her closet to find the right skimpy dress and killer heels.

Self-pity is pathetic, Michelle.

Desmond wheeled back so she could unbolt the door. "Hen. . ."

Henry blinked, as if he'd forgotten who she was or why he had come, then his pudding face widened in a grin. He knuckled her head, his greeting ever since he reached six feet four in middle school and she, a senior in high school, remained locked at four eleven. From then on, he seemed to think he was her big brother, beginning with stink-bombing Nic Sage's convertible after Nic stood up Michelle, July 4th, the summer before she left for college. When Desmond was born, Henry had moved downtown into her neighborhood "in case of emergency."

"Yo, Mich." His sleepy eyes and too-big chin made him look stupid, but he was a crack programmer for a gaming company. Spying Desmond behind her, he intoned, "It's Henrik, Prince Henrik zee Evil Von," and swatted her thigh with the Kurt's Krafts bag he carried, to make her get out of the way.

Desmond collapsed in paroxysms of delight. Henrik, a mash-up of Dr. Spock and a movie Nazi, was Desmond's favorite of Henry's many roles, which included a blind, lisping physical therapist, who would mistake Desmond's ear for his nose, a pirate, and some monsters who made weird sounds inspired by Henry's games. Desmond butted his wheelchair into the back of her legs and grabbed for the Kurt's bag, knowing it was for him.

Henry yanked it out of range. "Zees are for later, for za shower. Ve have un whole zoo." He handed Michelle the sack, grabbed the handles of Desmond's wheelchair, and careened down the hall toward the living room.

Inside the Kurt's bag she found a bunch of those capsules that dissolve in water and release spongy creatures. Grow animals. Desmond adored them. She tossed the bag in the bathroom—just once, she'd like a surprise for herself—and headed to the kitchen. A surprise for her? What a jerk. She paused at the hall mirror.

Lose the frowny face, Michelle.

In her early thirties, when her friends began to peel off into MarriedLand, and the unattached male herd began to thin, she had taken a serious look at her future and decided that what she wanted was a child, not marriage, not enduring coupledom. Her friends found her decision to be "totally cool," "courageous," "blasted awesome." But AD, these same friends had dropped away, their lives so different. How could they enjoy sharing their worries and aspirations for their children when confronted with Desmond? She was lucky to have a brother like Henry.

Lose the clown grin, Michelle.

She had a son she loved. She worked from home in a condo she could afford, had a decent job maintaining sales and inventory for TRAK-TEK, a company that sold used auto parts overseas. It wasn't her job BD—branding and marketing, make-a-bundle-spend-a-bundle, expensive parties and river cruises—but she could care for her boy. And every two weeks, when she went into the office, handsome Rivas in Systems, who never wore socks, not even in winter, and whose ankles were as beautiful as anything by Brancusi, he, Rivas, would say hello. Rivas, the married office flirt.

Michelle, you are pathetic.

Lasagna on the table, beer poured for Henry, milk in Desmond's sippy cup, her wine topped up, Michelle called them to the table.

Henry gorilla-grunted as he wheeled a sputtering and giggling Desmond to the table.

Her heart cracked open. Wishing her son's whole life could be all giggles, she strapped on his spork, tied on his "Da Boss" apron, and dished up the lasagna.

Henry loped around the table pawing his armpits.

"Settle down, Henry. You're egging Desmond on."

Both of them laughed at her, Desmond knocking his sippy cup sideways and Henry righting it. She asked if either of them would like salad, knowing they wouldn't, and the leftovers would be her lunch tomorrow.

"Salad, pallid, po bad it," Henry sang. "Nee naw no na nee."

Desmond sputtered out his first bite of lasagna. With her napkin she wiped his face and glared at Henry, who pretended to be chastened, then launched into a description of a new game someone, not he, was developing—time travel, massive weaponry, the usual.

Dinner was never pretty, but with Henry mimicking Desmond's jerky movements, tomato sauce and ricotta flew everywhere. At least Henry would shower Desmond afterward, a huge kindness. When Desmond graduated to a wheelchair, she'd taken out the tub, installed a walk-in, roll-in shower with a hand-spray, and bought a shower seat. Even so, bath times were increasingly difficult. He would twist and flay against the water's spray, sometimes bruising her. And he got erections. All boys do, the therapist said, even six-year-olds. What would she do when the hormones really kicked in?

She sipped her wine, half-listening as Henry droned on about medieval armor.

Desmond interrupted. "I want . . . knight . . . with . . . hose."

"Steed, Sir Desmond, a manly steed ye be wanting. Axel be his name."

"Axel, I like that name," Michelle said, picturing her son in full knight's regalia, upright and gallant in the saddle, his wheelchair having morphed into a black stallion, shaffron and crinet gleaming.

Desmond touched his chest with his curled hand. "Sir . . . Desmond." He pointed to her. "Mmm?"

"She be Maid Michelle."

"Not me." She downed the last of her wine. "Maid" was too accurate.

She went to the kitchen to retrieve the wine bottle. Two glasses—three actually—wouldn't be too much. She handed Henry a fresh beer.

He tipped back in his chair, took a long swig, and said, "Big news. A gamer's convention in Hong Kong, and I'll be there. Totally comped. With the fifteen-hour flight, makes sense to hang with some buddies in Jakarta after, and maybe swing by Bali."

Air squeezed from her lungs. He was abandoning her. "You in swim trunks?" she said.

He flat-eyed her as Desmond said, "I . . . swim."

"You're a dolphin, my man." Back to her. "I'll be gone six weeks, maybe longer."

Six weeks? She struggled to keep her face blank. Without Henry, she was alone.

Clingy is the public face of pathetic.

"Send us some pictures," she said, kicking back a slug of wine.

Henry said, "Des, my man, cover your ears. I want to talk privately"—he wiggled his eyebrows—"with your mom."

Desmond closed his eyes and began to hum as he patted the table with his spork-strapped hand, agreeably deserting her, too.

"I signed you up," Henry said, she could barely hear him over Desmond's racket, "with another dating site."

"Oh, shit, Henry." Her betraying baby brother. "Which email d'you use? I'll close it down."

"Fair Maid Michelle, you be live at this very moment."

"Asshole."

"Listen, Michelle," he leaned forward, his face looking sincerely stupid. "It's a site for single parents with special needs kids."

"A tragedy troll site? You really are the Evil One. Do they put little angels next to everyone's lying photos and extra angel wings for each disability your kid has? Dammit, Henry. I'm fine."

"You are forty-one, way too young to let your twat shrivel."

"You are disgusting. You are not allowed to know that I have a twat."

Desmond's eyes sprang open.

"Bath time," she almost shouted, reaching across the table to wipe tomato sauce from his chin. Too hard. He winced and she hated herself. "Sorry, buddy."

Henry said, "You'll be hearing from some men, which is better, admit it, better than the sound of . . ." he wiggled his eyebrows again, "the sound of silent tears."

"Eighth grade, right?" she said. "Wasn't that your theme song in eighth grade?"

Ignoring her, Henry unstrapped Desmond's spork, tugged off his apron, flipped off the brake lock, then turned the wheelchair toward the hall. "Sir Desmond, Maid Michelle needs a time out. You and I will see if we can grow you a manly steed."

"Asshole."

From the kitchen she listened to the squeals and splashes from the bathroom, her stomach curdling with self-pity, resenting that Henry's grow animals were a big hit. She slammed the dishwasher shut, glad that its loud grinding interrupted the sounds of happiness down the hall, and glanced at the wheelchair scuffs on the cabinets, then at the calendar with its irritating zigzag pattern. She ripped off the blue dots for Henry's visits and dropped them in the garbage.

Whatever site he'd found had to be a scam. For someone who earned his living in CyberLand, her brother could be remarkably naïve. Unattached men simply did not exist in the quote-unquote special parents club. She'd explained this to him, describing the dried up husks she encountered in her rounds with Desmond. Everyone, each and every man and woman, was withered, her too, which was why she'd decided to sign up with eHarmony. When she asked him to babysit, she'd told him in cringingly embarrassing detail—she'd drunk too much—that she wanted a man to tell her she was pretty; she wanted a man to touch her; she wanted her body to be the source of pleasure, again, and not simply a functional beast of burden. But in eHarmonyLand she found out that non-withered men do not want a woman who comes with a sidecar of responsibilities, responsibilities like a son who would always come first. When she came home from her last eHarmony fiasco, Henry's moon-face had sagged when she told him how the guy said he had to step outside the restaurant to take a call, and never came back. A good brother, her closest friend, but that didn't give him the right to mess in her business. Even if his site was legit, it had to be overwhelmingly full of lonely-hearts women. Most of the women in the special parents club were single-divorced, not like her, single-by-choice. Many men couldn't take a kid who would never grow up. Even if a miracle unattached man with a disabled kid did exist, he would be a dried-up husk, too: a punctilious planner, a worrier, never any craziness, and no goddamn fun. Just like her. She, who used to juggle men like oranges, would now be alone for the rest of her life.

Michelle, the road to stupid philosophizing is paved with drink, and you are drunk.

She opened her computer, ignored the flashing email icon—damn Henry—and entered TRAK TEK's portal. The dishwasher coughed and knocked. Down the hall the shower stopped. There were thumps and muffled laughter as Henry dried Desmond and carried him to his bedroom. Drawers slid open and closed, whispers, Henry's murmur reading a story. Blinking red lines announced that TRAK TEK's shipment to Singapore had been delayed in customs. She sent out a batch of notices to customers.

"Find anyone interesting?"

She jumped.

Henry stood in the doorway, his shirt spotted from Desmond's shower.

"I'm working." She returned her gaze to the spreadsheet on her computer screen, trusting her fury was visible.

"Mich, come on, you're my take-no-prisoners idol. I've built avatars based on you. Don't wimp out."

She snapped shut her computer. "It's not okay what you did. Admit it."

"Admit you're lonely."

"Admit you're a jerk."

He knuckled her head. "Good night, Mich."

She didn't walk him to the door.

After logging out, she—a pathetic mess, a self-pitying child who got bombed on watery, piss-colored wine—swayed down the hall, double-locked the front door, and slid the chain in place. The rattle of metal on metal, like a prison lock down. She pressed her face against the door and vowed she would never, ever drink again.

Down the hall the dishwasher shuddered to its stop. Quiet. All was quiet, so quiet she could hear her exhalation whisper on the door. She lifted her head. Through the open window in the living room came the tinkle of door chimes. Mr. G's, it had to be, across the street and four floors down. Then nothing. Silence. No ricocheted words, no car doors slamming, no screeching tires, bursts of laughter, no boom when a truck hit the metal plates that covered the sinkhole at the corner, not even the whine of the expressway two blocks over. She brushed her hair away from her ears, setting off waves of dizziness, but still hearing nothing. The rest of the world might have dropped away. She could be alone in the universe.

Desmond? She lurched toward his bedroom, needing to make sure he still existed. Into his dark room she tiptoed, watched by the red eye of his security camera. She paused, dizzied by the dancing spots of light that floated above him, from the revolving lamp on his nightstand, then walked closer. He was asleep, curled under his Batman quilt. Strands of damp hair clung to his forehead. Knotted fingers, wrists bent inward, arms that wouldn't straighten, legs like rubber bands, bent spine, and so small. Her beautiful birdboy. She slid his arm beneath his quilt, and he made a sweet sound.

With her hand on the wall to guide her, she padded down the hall. The bathroom was a mess, wheelchair parked by the toilet, wet towels and Henry's shoe prints all over the floor, and enormous animal sponges stuck to the shower tiles. No steed—broken promise, Bro?— but an orange camel the size of her laptop, a turtle as big as a basketball, a yellow pterodactyl with a wingspan the reach of her arms, far bigger than any grow animals she'd ever seen. Where had Henry gotten them? Not from Kurt's, that was for sure.

A black lump covered half the floor drain. She'd clean up in the morning. She flicked off the hall light, then back on, for Desmond.

In her dark bedroom, she flopped onto her bed, kicked off her slippers, tugged off her clothes, and rolled under the covers, her head swimming. A line of light from the hall sliced across her face, but she was too tired to get up and shut her door. She glanced at Desmond's monitor. His shadowy bed was just visible beneath the moving spots of light. The monitor buzzed.

Tomorrow you are going to have one monster headache.

Something wakes her.

Eyes closed, she listens to Desmond's monitor. Normal. She holds her breath, hearing nothing but the monitor's hum, remembering the eerie silence earlier, her and this apartment cut off from the world.

She blinks her eyes open. Something stands at her door, silhouetted in the hall's light, something blurry and dark, not exactly a shape, not as definite as a shape, not solid, but not transparent either. She must be dreaming. Or it is the wine? But she isn't afraid. Whatever it is hovers in her doorway, its head almost touching the door's lintel. It does have a head, but no face, not one that she can make out through her slit eyes, and a narrow body with arms that reach to where its knees would be if it had knees. The thing glides across the room toward her bed. She squeezes her eyes shut and listens to her heart knocking loud enough for whatever it is to hear. Still, strangely, she isn't afraid. The sheet above her flutters and lifts, admitting a chill puff of moist air that mists over her skin, prickling the tips of her breasts while, beneath her, the mattress shifts. Whatever it is has gotten into bed with her. It weighs less than a man would weigh. Pretending to sleep—maybe she is asleep—she smells something. Water? Has the dishwasher flooded? The bathroom? But there's no sloshing or dripping. And the scent that surrounds her isn't tinged with the ancient-iron-pipe tang of their water or Desmond's bubble-gum soap. It's pure and clean. Moisture suffuses the cells of her skin. Her whole body, muscles, bones, her too-tight skull, her spine that holds her upright through every day that she works so hard, all of her is softening. Deep within, she feels the old pulse of yearning. The creature nestles close and cradles her belly, its arm soft and damp and as spongy as a grow animal. She turns toward him, eyes closed, smiling. Clouds must smell like this, those boundless puffy clouds that drift without movement until they are gone.

Nature Rules

METAL SCREECHED, THE CHITTERING BIRDS stopped, then a thump: her bear, in the garbage that she'd dragged out to the road less than ten minutes ago. Bonnie grabbed her shotgun and hurried to the front door. At the end of her long driveway, trash trailed from the tipped-over can across the grass into the woods, the C-cure lid wobbled by the big oak, but her bear was gone. She fired skyward. Even if she got a bead on him, she would never shoot him. She and he—she was sure her bear was a he—they were engaged in a long-term game of mutual attention and respect. When the shotgun's echo died, she righted the can and gathered the debris as the garbage truck rumbled into view at the bend in the road. Eleven o'clock, right on time.

Lenn jumped from the cab, re-tying the bandanna around his neck—he thought he looked sexy—and said, "He's a sly one, that bear. You got the best can, best lid, these things"—he batted the useless bungee cords as he dumped her garbage—"and you keep it locked up. Only thing left is to quit making garbage."

"Us humans, we make garbage, but I'm doing my best. Does he get into the Levitskys' or the Nelsons'?" Her neighbors up the road, whose houses weren't visible, even in the winter when the deciduous trees were bare.

"I'd say Mr. Bear likes you, Miss Bonnie. You got that special, single woman thing going."

"Come on, Lenn."

"Fancy cheese wrappers, smoked trout, maybe, nice smelling shampoo and body wash." He stretched out "body wash."

"Give it a rest, Lenn." Lenn, married, with six kids under ten, was the island flirt.

"You get scared of Mr. Bear, you call me." He mimed phone-to-ear as he jumped back into the cab.

"I'll call Vardeen first." His wife.

"Spoil sport." He laughed and waved as he drove off.

That's what Bonnie loved about this place: everyone had a take-it-in-stride attitude. Bear in the garbage. Bats. Mice drowning in the bucket under the leaky sink. Snow-bound winters. Frozen pipes. *Nature rules,* islanders said.

She'd moved north to the island two years ago, after her mother died and left her twenty thousand dollars. She'd wanted a new life, far from her kids, her crummy job in the county clerk's office, and her mother's depressing house on Chicago's north side, which she'd also inherited and where the kids, or at least Sadie lived, and where Milo came to recover each time he messed up. Training racehorses in Florida, he knew nothing about horses; organic farming in Missouri, a pot farm, probably, where the farmer refused to pay him, so he said; living on the beach in Kauai, where he panhandled for food. Milo had taken so much out of her. Sadie, too, always thinking she knew better than Bonnie how to do just about everything. A different life, that's what Bonnie wanted, and some distance. The island, a day's drive from Chicago, but a million miles away, was no vacation destination. Working quarries, managed forests, three taverns, the gas station/grocery store where she worked part-time, a post office, a medical clinic open one afternoon a week, all near the ferry dock. The only paved roads led from the dock to the quarries and the gated entrance to the forest. She bought a house eight miles out on a dirt road and, in the first six months, had been frightened by every sound. She bought a .410 shotgun, took lessons, practiced with soup cans on the stump out back. She learned to chop wood, plow her driveway, and thwack a scythe through the brush at the edge of the ever-encroaching woods. *You don't fight back, the woods will reclaim your place in a year,* that's what everyone said.

She set her shotgun on her kitchen counter and walked toward the sliding glass doors that overlooked her deck and the woods beyond.

She'd seen the bear just once. A sunny day. She'd been standing at these glass doors, and a black shape, big as the meat freezer in her garage, glided through the un-mown grass between her deck and the edge of the woods. The upper edge of the thing, a moving line, head and spine, she realized later, glistened with sunlight, even though the shape was so black that it looked like an inexplicable gap torn in the familiar. When it was gone, she understood it had been a bear. She waited for him to reappear, wanting to feel again the eerie thrill of his presence, but for days, she'd been too scared to go into her backyard. *You got nothing to fear from bears, if you're no threat,* everyone said.

She touched the glass, watching the woods. That's where he was now, maybe watching her.

The phone rang.

"Mom, what are you doing?" Sadie.

"My bear's been in the garbage again." Bonnie fixed her eyes on the aspens behind her target stump.

"Listen, Mom, I need to talk to you. It's about Milo." Sadie always spoke about her brother in a superior, big sister way, although they were only a year apart. Twenty-seven and twenty-six. Irish twins, Bonnie's mother had called them, disapproving of two births so close together and Bonnie not married. Blaming Sandro for that, and for hijacking Bonnie to the godforsaken farm in Ontario. And blaming Bonnie, forever, when Sandro deserted her.

"Mom, promise me you won't look up what Milo did on the Internet."

Milo on the Internet? Witchy fingers threaded through Bonnie's gut. "I don't have the Internet," she said, keeping her voice calm. "A storm knocked out my connection."

Sadie told her to sit down. Bonnie lied, said she was sitting as she remained at the sliding glass doors watching a dragonfly big as a hummingbird land on the coffee mug she'd left out by her deck chair.

"Milo's been arrested. Eleven felony counts so far."

Bonnie closed her eyes and pressed her forehead to the glass. Was he dealing again?

Sadie talked about a van, a rental van, Nashville.

"Nashville?" Eleven felonies. How could that be?

"He thought he'd get into the music scene." Sadie paused, waiting for Bonnie to say something. When she didn't, Sadie went on. Milo didn't have a credit card. You need a credit card to rent a van. He got angry, beat up the guy, took keys, stole a van, crashed into a Payless shoe store, broke into two houses, then beat up an old man. "He kicked an old man, Mom. Milo kicked an old man walking to church on Sunday morning."

Sunday? What was today? She looked at the calendar on the pillar near the kitchen, trying to breathe. It must be Tuesday. Why hadn't Sadie called her sooner? Needing air, she slid open the glass door. The dragonfly was gone. Birds cried, two of them, call and response, and the wind ruffled the aspens. Any light breeze could set the aspens dancing.

"Where is he now?" she asked. Her blue-eyed boy. Eleven felonies. This wouldn't be like the time he stole the car. She'd gotten him off, but then he was sixteen. Or the time he lit a fire in the psych ward, when Bonnie's attorney got him off by threatening the hospital with a negligence suit.

"The police have him. In Louisville."

"Louisville or Nashville? I thought—"

"He was going to Nashville. Mom, are you getting any of this?"

"Where are you?"

"At home. Milo called me." She meant, You're his mother, he should have called you.

"What was he doing in Louisville?"

"Good god, Mom. He's been living in Louisville for six months."

Bonnie didn't even know where her son was living. The last time they'd talked was two months ago, maybe more. He'd phoned to ask for three grand to buy a couch. When she'd protested, he'd said, "This is a fresh start." How many times had she heard this? "Great," she remembered saying, she always tried to stay positive, "but why do you need a three thousand dollar couch?" Then he ranted. She didn't understand, she didn't care. How could he make something of himself if he lived in a homeless shelter? No, he wasn't living in a shelter. He'd found an apartment. He was applying for jobs. Why couldn't she see that he needed nice things? She asked if he was taking his meds. He hung up. She'd been worried but persuaded herself he'd call when he was ready. Not hearing from him was good. He was, after all, twenty-six.

"I'll drive down," she said to Sadie. "Tell me where to go. I'll see what can be done."

"Come here. We'll go together."

Bonnie said she'd catch the first ferry in the morning and arrive in Chicago around three, three thirty. After she hung up, she closed the glass door, shutting out the bird sounds and breeze, feeling as if the lid had been lowered on her coffin.

She phoned RJ at the store. Could he find someone to cover for her for a few days, maybe a week? Family emergency. Sure, he could make do. He was shaking his head, Bonnie knew, commiserating. Everyone here was kind.

In the closet behind her suitcase, she saw the box storing the old videos. The player was long gone, but she hadn't thrown out the tapes. She didn't need to play them to remember.

The video opens with a green swath, the grass in her mother's backyard. Bonnie is holding the camera. The image tips up to find a blurry Milo squatting beside the sandbox while Sadie's four-year-old voice squeals at Bonnie to hurry. A frog. A frog. The picture bounces as Bonnie hurries toward Milo with Sadie's hand entering the frame to wave her forward. Don't touch it. Mommy's coming.

In late afternoon, after she'd packed and put up the storm windows, a job she'd planned for next week, she heard a car in her driveway. It didn't reverse out. She went to the window and saw a dark sedan with a heavy man standing beside the open driver's door. Wanting directions? Interested in buying her black walnut trees? He lifted his hand to shield his eyes from the low sun and hitched his shoulders in a familiar way. Sandro? Sandro, thickset and old? She'd never imagined him aging. She ducked back—he couldn't have seen her—and reached for her shotgun. Edging close to the window again, she watched him straighten and turn slowly to shut the car door. What was he now, fifty-six? Twenty-four years ago was the last time she'd seen him, when he'd put her and the kids, Milo still nursing, on the train south to Detroit, then on to Chicago, to stay at her mother's. He was to join them in two weeks, after he helped Clary sell the livestock and ready the farm for winter. When he didn't come and didn't come, Bonnie had believed he'd been hurt or kidnapped or lost his memory, was wandering in some urban hell or locked up in a charity hospital or a jail cell. When Clary finally answered the phone, she said Sandro had taken his share of the livestock proceeds and left, saying something about Vancouver. "But he's supposed to come here, to me," Bonnie had protested. After an interminable silence, Clary had said she didn't know anything about that.

Now here Sandro was, standing in her driveway looking at her home. Jeans, dark shirt, boots, much the same, but heavier, his hair, dark and long-ish, like he was still trying to get women.

She propped the gun against the doorjamb, in reach—she wasn't going to make a fool of herself—and waited. At his knock, she opened the door. "What the hell are you doing here?"

"Hello, Bonnie." The maritime accent she'd forgotten.

She shocked him, she could tell, even though his expression didn't change. Had he expected the smooth-faced, compliant girl she'd once been? Now her skin was freckled and her brown hair salted with gray and short, no longer twisted into a braid that reached to her waist. Not bad for forty-eight, but she wished she looked better, to make him regret, and was furious at herself. Behind his thickened face—he probably drank too much—she could make out the ghost of the younger, handsome Sandro, ready to charm.

"What the hell are you doing here?" she repeated, holding the door. What she'd planned to say to him if she ever saw him again, the complaints and questions that she'd rehearsed and refined over all those years in the back bedroom of her mother's house, adding new charges as the kids got older—and he not there—all that was gone. She had nothing to say to him, and she sure as hell didn't want to hear what he had to say. The absence of explanation had become a comfort. The void of reason, that made sense.

He glanced at the shotgun in the shadows beside her. "You shoot strangers?" He was amused, she could see. A gun? She'd hated the guns on the farm, hated the fall slaughter, hated even the killing of hens for the stew pot.

"There's a bear," she said.

He nodded, uninterested, and studied her. He could look all he wanted and see nothing true about her. He inhaled and flexed his shoulders, as if preparing to say why he'd come. She crossed her arms to say she didn't care.

"It's Milo," he said.

He knew. How the hell? She willed her expression to give nothing away. "What does that have to do with you?" Sadie must have found him. The damned Internet. Sandro wouldn't have gone looking for them. Milo had to have been in on it, too. They, her children, had kept this from her. For how long?

"Sadie asked me to come," Sandro said. "Believe me, I'm here for one reason only, for Milo and Sadie."

"For Milo and Sadie? After not caring all the years when they cried every night for you." Or when Sadie refused to go to kindergarten, or the year when the cool girls shunned her, or the time she broke her leg. Or when Milo had such a hard time losing his baby teeth and his one incisor never came, or when the calls from the school began and the run-ins with the cops, the drugs, the string of alternative schools, his dropping out altogether, the hellish business with the psych ward. "You know nothing about the kids. You abandoned them."

Milo looks up, his little moon face pinched with nervousness and excitement. When he sees her, he bends forward, picks up a lump, lurches to his feet, and runs toward her, his stubby legs churning. She's knelt on the grass to steady the camera and waits. He holds the frog smack in front of his chest, so proud, clutching it with both hands. A few feet in front of her, he trips and falling, he thrusts the frog at her, the frog's head filling the frame, its mouth stretched wide, shooting out red, gouts of blood, as Milo squeezes the life out of it. A plunge to green as Bonnie drops the camera to reach for her blue-eyed boy.

"Jeesuz-H-Christ, Bonnie." Sandro ran his fingers through his hair in the way that had once made her melt. Her gut clenched. "Listen, we have to talk. Can I come in?"

She wanted to pick up the gun and bash his face, but she reached behind her with a stiff arm and closed the door.

"We can talk out here." She didn't want him in her house, looking at her things and making assumptions about her.

He stepped back a few feet, maintaining the distance between them, and peered up at the expanse of siding that she'd re-stained herself in the heat of July.

"This isn't where I thought you'd end up," he said.

His smugness infuriated her. "Sadie's calling on you is pathetic and desperate. She's confused you with a real father. Say what you came to say and get going."

His nostrils flared. "You've got a rulebook, don't you, Bonnie, a fucking rulebook. You've gone from being a needy, play-by-the-rules girl, love-marriage-baby carriage-rules, to a self-righteous . . . what's the word?"

"Woman? Grown-up woman?"

"Christ. Okay, I didn't operate by your rulebook, but there's more than one way of looking at things. Don't forget that. I'm here, right this goddamn minute, because you and I need to talk before seeing Sadie, and Milo. If they'll let us see Milo."

Us? "Have you seen them in the last two decades?"

"No."

He turned away, his gaze traveling beyond the corner of her house to the woods. At the edge of her yard, behind the stunted pine, she felt a presence. Her bear, she guessed, watching her now with this stranger. Had he felt Sandro's threat?

" . . . I'm not saying—"

"Not saying what? That you screwed them and me? This now, with Milo, has nothing to do with you. I'm driving down in the morning. I'll handle it, like I've—"

"Do I have to say again that Sadie asked me to help? She asked me to talk to you and to come. I'm here because our children asked me. You better believe that you're about the last . . . " An ugly red flushed his cheeks. He shoved his hands in his pockets and exhaled. "Sadie doesn't need any of your shit making this even harder. When I got her call, I was on the road. She gave me this address, and your number, but I knew you wouldn't pick up the phone if you saw my name."

Sadie was a traitor.

He walked to the porch railing. "I have to get back to the Cities tonight, that's where I live, but I'll drive south by mid-afternoon, should arrive by late tomorrow at Sadie's house."

"The house belongs to me. That's where I raised them, without you. My mother left the house to me."

He said nothing, shifting to face away. She was being petty, that's what he meant. That she'd raised the children on her own: that was irrelevant. She snapped her fingers. That was all any of it meant to him. At the sound of her fingers snapping, he turned, but she looked past him. Shadows had crept from the woods. Above the fringed top of the trees, the tip of the tallest spruce caught the slanting rays of the sun and glowed like polished brass. In there somewhere her bear was watching.

"I'm not sure if we'll be able to see Milo," Sandro said.

"Why couldn't we?" Why had she said we?

"Bonnie, it's cold. Can we talk inside?"

The wind had kicked up, swaying the grass beyond the porch. She shivered. A few times in the summer, she'd seen a trail of trampled grass circling her house, her bear keeping an eye on her. She knows where he sleeps: in the crushed ferns next to the tip-up, in the patch of broken Indian pipes under the beech, and on the far bank of the creek near her property line. Never has she seen any other sign of him, no scraps of her garbage dragged into the woods, no small half-eaten carcasses left behind. Her bear is immaculate. His life is clean.

She could sense him gazing at her.

Sandro shifted his weight, startling her. She said, "I'll meet you at. . . Did you see that bar, right outside of town on the left, the Island Oasis? I'll meet you there in a half hour."

He locked his eyes on hers.

She looked through him, to what was ahead. The emphasis would shift from Milo's disaster to Sandro's arrival. The father returning to save the day would replace the disappearing dad. She would be the old grind; he would be the wondrous savior.

"I'll be there," she said to Sandro.

Off camera, Bonnie reaches for Milo to hug him close as the videotape records a tangle of grass. His flailing fists, his body fighting to twist away from her, his wild heart pounding against hers, all this goes unrecorded, as do his shrieks, "Don't want you. Want my daddy. My daddy."

Sandro backed out of her driveway, the headlights switching on.

She walked through the house, the sight of her fat couch, the lamps she'd made from dairy cans, the smell of fireplace ash comforting her. She had created a whole new life. She imagined Sadie phoning to say that Milo had not done whatever he'd done, it was all an ugly joke, and she was sorry. Or Sandro might disappear again. Or have a heart attack. Or Bonnie could. She put two fingers on her neck and felt the pulse of her stupidly reliable heart. Then she brought in the mug she'd left on the deck, closed the windows, washed her face, splashing her shirt, not caring, and stuffed her wallet and keys into her jacket. Outside the night air was cold and crisp, the moon just visible to the east.

She had come this far to get away, and it wasn't far enough.

Her boots caught in the grass as she walked past her target-practice stump. If her bear were anywhere near, he would understand in the way that animals understand that she was no threat. *You got nothing to fear from bears, if you're no threat.* She just needed a few minutes to breathe unsullied air. At the edge of the woods, she turned to look back at her house, her kitchen lamp shining through the glass doors.

At the Island Oasis Sandro would be settling in, a Black Russian in front of him, chatting with Lucien behind the bar, or trying to charm the deadbeats who hung out there in the middle of the week. If she left now, he wouldn't have cause to check the time and think she was being difficult.

Brambles snagged her jeans as she stepped into the forest. Ahead, all was shades of black and silent, the small animals gone quiet. Even the dumbest creatures know to dive for cover when menaced. They couldn't know that she was no menace. She held her breath. No wind, no rustling, no bear pushing through the underbrush.

In a while, Sandro would be annoyed. He'd mask that, charmer that he was, ordering another silly girls' drink, or several, and in an hour, he'd realize that she wasn't coming, toss money on the bar, and drive out here to berate her. No. He had to get back to the Cities. He'd phone Sadie, tell her that Bonnie had refused to cooperate, and Sadie would think, as she always did, that Bonnie was a lousy mother. Even so, they would expect her to show up tomorrow.

And she might. She could sleep next to the tip-up, where the moss was thick and spongy, and in the morning, brush off the leaves she'd used for a blanket. She could catch the first ferry.

Or her bear might come for her. Would that be so bad? To die? To be free of the entangling feelings that had snared her since Sandro appeared, since Sadie called, since Milo began screwing up, since the beginning? Her bear would be quick. Skin flailed, muscle torn, bones broken, pain, excruciating pain, but over in a flash. Then . . . nothing. Such ease it would be to feel nothing.

She was tired of it all, tired of human beings, tired of being human. Nearby the little animals began to rustle and click. What they and her bear had was what she wanted: a constant present, no past, no future, all of that absent, only this inhalation, this heartbeat, this moment.

When she didn't show up in Chicago, they would . . . what? They would have to travel to where Milo was, angry with her, but not worried, focused on Milo. With Sandro there would they even need her? In a week, maybe two, Sadie would phone RJ and he'd call the cops. They would find her kitchen light on and her car in the garage. They might think she'd gone off with someone. They'd ask questions of the Levitskys and the Nelsons, they'd check with the kids who worked the ferry. When that came up bust, they would search the woods. Her boots, shredded clothes, keys, skull, shattered bones. A tragedy, Sadie and Milo would be told. *Nature rules.*

Taking a deep breath, she stumbled forward, a vine grazing her shoulder, her eyes straining to see. In the distance from the dark, a black patch broke free and thundered toward her. Branches thrashing, ground shaking, roaring everywhere in her head, veins, limbs, everywhere. She waited, terrified, eyes shut, hoping it wasn't a deer.

Call Back

EUGENE STUDIED HIS FACE IN the mirror, the pouches beneath his eyes, the fleshy jowls, and saw himself as young, maybe thirty-five, thin and lantern-jawed, in fact, as Tom Courtenay playing Norman in *The Dresser.*

This morning the part of Norman will be played by Eugene Meltzer.

Twenty years ago, no, more, it had been since he'd seen Courtenay on the London stage. The effect of Courtenay's performance as the repressed servant frustrated by rage and absurd love for his master had thrilled Eugene. He hunched his shoulders forward, mimicking Courtenay's half-lowered eyes, his cheeks flattened like armored face plates. He turned to three-quarter profile and glowered at the mirror, unable to remember who'd played opposite—Courtenay had been so intense that he'd blotted out everything else on the stage—and flexed one nostril, trying for menace, then snorted at his vanity. Not even in his youth had he been able to pull off any kind of intense. Now he'd gone soft, put on weight, lost too much hair, just right for supporting roles. Perfect for the role of servant. Turning from the mirror, he picked up Glenna's tray, balanced it against the mound of his belly, and shuffled toward the living room. In the entryway, he paused.

Interior, small apartment, living room, dimly lit. Stage left: a green bro-cade armchair, the worse for the wear, flanked by a floor lamp and a small dark wood table, crowded with Kleenex, small stuffed animals, a drinking glass sprouting an angled straw, a large TV tuned to a shopping channel. Through curtains, bay window stage rear, faint morning light falls in a bro-ken pattern on a worn oriental rug. Slowly, a spotlight brightens in front of the armchair and illuminates a pair of furry bedroom slippers, big as cats, then widens to include the pajama-clad legs of an old woman sitting in the chair. Stooped, too thin, with shoulder-length, silky white hair. She is wear-ing a pink cardigan sweater over pajamas. She gives no sign of hearing him enter. She gives no sign of watching the brassy blonde on the TV. She gives no sign at all.

On Glenna's good days, he could be Gielgud in *Arthur*, the proper, silly butler, and participate in the madness, but not with the onset of No-vember and the clanging radiators and Glenna raging that he had stolen her clothes; all that drew him to the dark, claustrophobic world of *The Dresser*.

"Glenna," he said, with a British accent, nudging aside the Kleenex box and the Beanie Babies on the side table to clear a space for the tray, "I'll be leaving soon."

Her hand plucked at her pajama leg, a pecking bird, but her eyes re-mained fixed on the TV. The musty, over-ripe fruit smell of her exhalation wafted around him.

"It's time for your medicine," he said. "Afterward"—she stuck out her tongue—"afterward"—he placed the Aricept in the center of her white-flannelled tongue—"I'll brush your hair." Carefully, he tipped the glass upward and watched her swallow. Sometimes her compliance seemed less like acquiescence than a taunt: "You can't touch me." He wiped away a dribble and muttered that she was a good girl.

She nodded, then her forehead knit with exasperation. "Tell that fool on lights that he's supposed to follow me until I exit."

"I'll take care of it."

"I smell . . ." Her chin trembled, and she looked up at Eugene. "What is it I smell?" she asked, her voice high and querulous.

Nothing, that's what the doctors told him after she left the gas burner on without a flame; she could smell nothing. He touched her cheek. "It's *'I smell jonquils.'*"

She repeated her line from *The Glass Menagerie.* They'd been married about a year, when she starred in the Guthrie's production. Had her pick of roles and he, twelve years her junior, was just starting out. Not that he'd gotten very far.

"Glenna, I have to go soon."

She looked past him, toward the TV, squeezing her hands between her thighs, and started to chuckle. "If you touch my purse, I'll have you fired."

Mimicking Norman's long-suffering gait, Eugene retrieved her empty purse from the bedroom and held it in her field of vision. She snatched it, clutched it to her chest, and smiled as if she'd bested him. Yesterday, he'd found her purse wedged between the mattress and the box springs, stuffed with underpants, the framed 8x10 of her as Lettice Douffet, and his missing keys.

"Let me brush your hair before I go," he said, in his own voice, tired of games.

"No," she shrieked. "Eugene always does my hair."

He seized her chin, forcing her to look up at him. "Goddamn it, Glenna, I'm Eugene."

Fright widened her eyes, then slipped away, leaving her expression empty. He imagined a cornfield, a gunshot, an explosion of birds, then everything settling back, and the silence that followed. Thrilled and ashamed, he released her.

With sickening docility, she bent her neck. Reviling himself, Eugene picked up the brush and gently stroked her hair.

"I have an audition downtown. For a commercial. I'll be back by mid-afternoon."

In the kitchen, he rinsed out the glass, put away the tray, took the knobs off the stove, tied the handles of the refrigerator and freezer together with a tea towel, made sure the paring knife he'd used to clean their cantaloupe was back with the other knives, out-of-reach above the cabinets. Sink empty, back door locked, keys in his pocket, a plastic tumbler on the counter.

Down one flight of stairs, he tapped on Carmella's door and said he would be back by three o'clock. If not, he'd call. Lunch was in the refrigerator.

Carmella dipped her head, tugging her ponytail out of baby Ramon's fist as he struggled on her hip. "No worry. I go up right. She a fine lady. We be fine."

Buoyed with gratitude, for sweet Carmella, for being able to get away, for the rain holding off, for having a shot at a job, he hurried for the El. This was his first audition in eight months. By the time he reached the Fine Arts building, he was breathless with nerves. *All Passes, Art Alone Remains* read the bronze inscription on the lobby's arch. His agent had said the thirty-second spot was for Advil. On the ninth floor, he pushed open the wooden door with frosted window.

Half a dozen men lost in their own thoughts slump in worn orange chairs. Overhead fluorescents, stained ceiling tiles, faded travel posters hanging askew on the walls. A couple of nineteen-fifties table lamps, one door opposite, to the inner sanctum.

It could be the set for Sartre's *No Exit*. And it was definitely low budget. Not Advil. "Like Advil," that's what his agent had said.

Adjusting his hopes downward, Eugene nodded to Mike Sherr, Jim Poole, Sy Ziminsky, Lou Leggett, Harry Meeks, and three others he didn't know. Harry inclined his head toward the empty chair on the other side of the corner table. Hiding his reluctance, Eugene sat down and rummaged in his overcoat for a tissue. He hadn't seen Harry in more than a year and a half, not since *The Sea Gull* when Harry played the lead, Trigorin, naturally, while Eugene was the hapless Dorn.

"The script?" Eugene indicated the sheet of paper that Harry was folding into an accordion.

"The girl'll give you one. Basically, you suffer in your sleep, act annoyed when your wife makes you take the 'product'—that's what it says—and wake happy, like you've had a good fuck."

"I'd have to fake it," someone said, as Lou Leggett slapped down *Newsweek*. "I'll buy it, whatever it is."

Eugene wiped his nose to hide his discomfort. What had it been, five years, since the last time?

"How is she?" Harry asked.

A goddamn mind reader. "The same."

The last time he'd been able to take Glenna anywhere except the clinic was during *The Sea Gull*'s run, and Harry had been a prince, that was Harry all over, a real prince, sitting with her backstage, gossiping. Not that she understood a word. Eugene calculated backward; eighteen years it was since Harry and Glenna had that fling they thought he didn't know about.

Harry scrunched his eyes earnestly. "You know, I was reading about—"

"Sy Ziminski." A stocky girl in a skirt short enough to show off a Betty Boop tattoo on her thigh held open the inner door. Glad for the interruption, Eugene stood and apologized for being late. "No problem," she said, handing him the script. From the inner sanctum came a bark of laughter.

To shut Harry up, Eugene made a show of searching for his reading glasses and stared at the script.

Man: In bed, tossing and turning, struggles to sit, gives up and calls to wife. "Honey. I can't sleep."

Harry said something. Eugene lowered the paper and tightened his cheeks slightly to telegraph his forbearance.

"—holding up?"

Back to Glenna. "I'm handling it." He turned back to the script.

"Did you see the item about new retirement place for actors—"

"No."

"It was in the newsletter."

"Not in our budget." Their current rent of six hundred and fifty dollars was a struggle. Leaking faucets, plaster buckling under the living room window, electrical outlets that sparked. He pictured the overloaded adapter in their bedroom, behind the TV table. Had he forgotten to unplug it?

"Come on. Glenna had some good years," Harry said. "Surely you socked something away?"

Apprehensive, looking through Harry, Eugene remembered bending to fetch Glenna's childish slippers. And reaching for the plug. Relieved, he focused on Harry's carefully trimmed eyebrows and slipped into Norman. "Not enough to cover us living apart," he said, smarmily, but withholding a concluding "sir."

"It's worth looking into, for gods' sakes. I don't know, maybe Medicare . . ." Good old Harry, always the know-it-all. Harry leaned forward. "All I'm saying is it's worth a look."

Eugene grunted and looked at his script, the words indistinct gray smudges, determined not to let Harry derail him. He wanted this job. He fixed on the letters until they stopped moving. *Honey. I can't sleep.* He mouthed the words, hearing in his head an elongated nasal bleat. Not that. He relaxed his lips and silently ran through the line again. *Ho—ney*, two long syllables.

"God, not that, Eugene," Glenna had insisted on their first night together when he'd called her honey. "It's too banal. And no darling, or baby, or sweetie. No kumquat, chouchou, cupcake. No pet endearments of two syllables. No lovebug, honeypot—"

"That's three syllables."

"I do like an actor who knows his math," she'd said, wiggling her cold toes upward toward his crotch. He'd gasped and stared at the stolen "Men at Work" sign on the wall above her bed, trying to divert himself from the certainty that he didn't belong with this woman. She took pity and lifted her foot, drawing him close. "Okay. No baby, darling, sweetie, and no reference to food in any form, especially and emphatically honey."

"What do you leave me then?" he'd moaned, stirring against her belly, his eyes still locked on the sign's rusted yellow corner.

"Try 'glass.' You can say, 'Glenna Glass' and I'll know just what you mean."

The door to the inner room opened and the audition girl signaled for Jim Poole. One by one the others were called. Last to arrive, Eugene would be last called. "You've got my number, Eugene. Be in touch," Harry said when he came out. Eugene lied, saying he would.

When it was his turn, he hid his dismay at the sight of three bored young men. The one with spiky hair nodded for Eugene to begin, while the one in the tie shoved papers into a briefcase. Eugene adjusted his shoulders and smiled. A pro does not walk out. A pro does not say fuck it. The girl with the Betty Boop tattoo spoke the wife's first line. He gave a smooth reading, an excellent reading; he *was* an aggrieved, uncomfortable husband. *What am I going to do-ooo?* The director thanked him without meeting his eye.

In the empty waiting room, Eugene stared at a cruise ship sailing up a cyan fiord. Soon his agent would quit sending him out. There were open calls, of course. New theater groups kept springing up, all staffed by the kids whose choice of plays seldom included parts for the likes of him. What he had to look forward to was playing one last role, which, to be fair, he was free to interpret in various ways—one part, that of caretaker to the woman who was also his only audience, and she, god bless her, was incapable of judging. No, he was exaggerating. His audience wasn't only Glenna; it included the JCC's shuttle bus driver, Carmella and her family, the staff at the clinic, the occasional, distant, bumbling friend who phoned, unaware.

Outside on the sidewalk, he adjusted his scarf against the wind. Where could he sit in peace without having to pay three bucks for a cup of coffee? It was past two o'clock and Carmella would be expecting him, but he couldn't bring himself to go home. Turning north, he saw the Art Institute.

His knees ached as he threaded his way up the wind-whipped stairs, past *Streetwise* vendors and gaggles of schoolchildren. Inside, a guard waved him in. Tuesday, No Admission Fee. On the Grand Staircase he paused in the cool, filtered light from the skylights as throngs streamed past him toward the Impressionists' galleries. He took the opposite stairs, toward the old European wing, which, he guessed, would be empty. No one was interested in the old.

In his twenties, when he was always, it seemed, looking for work, he would kill time in the Art Institute. Not that he had much interest in art. But it was quiet and free. In those days, you could set off a cannon without hurting anyone. The grimy skylights shed a perpetual twilight. In that undisturbed calm, everything else fell away, the outside world, the hubbub, all his worries. "What did I have to worry about then?" he muttered, recalling how he would stroll, lost in his own thoughts, stopping now and then to examine an Albright or a Rothko. When his legs gave out, he would find a bench.

He pulled open tall doors, happy to see two unoccupied benches and hurried into the vast, nearly empty hall. A couple of middle-aged Asian tourists nodded at one of the immense paintings, and in the farthest corner, a grizzled, elderly man stood. Eugene sat down and massaged his knees, grateful for the stillness, and relaxed. He liked being surrounded by silent noblemen and saints he didn't believe in, scenes as illusory as anything he'd ever acted in. It would all outlast him. The thought comforted him. Even when he was young, when what he loved about acting was its perpetual present tense, the endurance of art shored him up. Why had he quit coming? He rooted in his pockets for a Kleenex, knowing the answer. It was marriage; it was the no longer being alone.

A couple of teenage girls shrieked in front of him, pointing at one of the paintings on the far wall. "Omigod, that guy has cut out his own tongue!"

"Gross."

The shorter girl pranced back. "We could take a picture and send it to Father Pat and maybe he'd get the idea to quit all his yakking . . ."

Glenna used to chatter morning to night, about any trivial thing, the necklace snagged on her sweater, lines of dialogue, swearing at stuck jar lids. Eugene fought a wash of grief; when he opened his eyes, the girls were gone. He stood and walked toward the canvas that had shocked them, but paused, turning toward a different painting, one sixteen feet tall or more, shimmering from the skylight's reflection. He shifted position to see through the glare. Near the top of the painting, a young angel, incandescent with fury, scowled down on a chaotic close-quarters fight scene. The angel's light, hot as a stage spot, blasted everything else into near obscurity: the flailing Roman soldiers, the fallen helmets, the dropped swords, the beaked and scrawny old man in a loincloth watching from the edge. Justice was being served. The iniquity of the world, its unfairness and humiliation and shame, were being avenged. The angel's flowing white radiance poured into Eugene. His heart beat noisily as he reached out and held his fingers inches from the varnished surface, wanting to touch the light that fled beneath his hand's shadow.

"It's a fake," said a voice.

Eugene jerked back. A thick hand missing the ring finger stabbed at the wall label. It was the old man who'd been at the far end of the gallery. "They claim it's a Caravaggio," he said, his breath sour with tobacco, "but it's not."

Eugene put on his glasses to read the label. "Francesco Buoneri, 'Ceccio' de Caravaggio, a follower of Caravaggio." He'd always liked Caravaggio and Giotto and Cimabue, names he'd once practiced under an accent coach for a bit part in a mob movie.

"Caravaggio," Eugene whispered, unfurling the syllables like a banner. "The Resurrection." He straightened, the word "fake" floated into his mind. He turned, prepared to brush off the old man. No one was there. The shadowless light swelled, then dimmed. For a moment, nothing seemed real or solid. A cloud blocking the sun, Eugene told himself, uncertain. Shaken, he stared up at the painting.

Downstairs, at the information desk, he asked a woman if the Art Institute owned any genuine Caravaggios. If "The Resurrection" was the handiwork of an imitator, he wanted to see the genuine article. "No," the woman said, shaking her head, "they're quite rare."

Disappointed, he walked out into the cold. It was already dark. By the time he rounded the corner of their block it was after five. As he reached the outer glass door, something moved behind the inner door. Someone leaving, he assumed as he scrounged for his keys, then glimpsed a pale hand pull away. Glenna's hand. He rushed forward, fumbling with the lock. Glenna cowered in the stairwell, naked. Her icicle ankles rose from her furry blue slippers. Her hands were clasped in front of her flaccid belly. Gray-white skin hung from her thighs like soggy wrappings. From upstairs came the sound of rushing water and someone yelping, "no, no, no."

He twisted out of his overcoat, furious and afraid, draping it over Glenna's shoulders, and urged her forward, the din filling his head. He tugged her up the stairs, past her clothes strewn on the landing, one more flight, through their open door, toward the racket: Carmella sobbing at their kitchen sink, washing blood from her baby's hand. She flung out her hand. Water drops hit Eugene's chest. Glenna had stabbed Ramon with scissors.

Shutting Glenna in their bedroom, Eugene dug out all the cash he had, two twenties and some singles, and thrust it at Carmella, saying he'd pay for the hospital, as she rushed for the door, with Ramon's hand swaddled in paper towels.

"Two stitches," she told him later that night. And she wouldn't be coming back. "You keep her away."

❖

Eugene made phone calls. He called the place mentioned in the union newsletter, the social worker at the JCC, the doctor's office. The prices they quoted were way out of his league. On Friday, with Glenna at adult daycare, Eugene went to the library to research options. He asked the kind, myopic librarian for help. She pushed her swivel chair away from the desk and handed him a thick black binder spilling brochures. "This should get you started."

Grateful not to be sent to the Internet terminals, he found an empty table and flipped through the binder's contents: newspaper articles, press releases, flyers showing white-haired people playing cards, peering at computer screens with a helpful attendant, smiling from lawn chairs in dappled gardens. In spite of his certainty that this was all beyond their means, optimism crept up on him. He began taking notes about staff-to-client—client?—ratios, Alzheimer patient services, fee structures and buy-in shares. At the bottom of the column on costs, he drew a big question mark. Social Security, a small annuity, and fifteen thousand in the bank; that was it. That's what he had to show for five decades as an actor, that, and a suitcase of yellowed notices. What little he'd been able to stockpile came from industrials and voice-overs, not exactly the career he'd projected. Glenna had done better. Broadway, some film work, lucrative, but all spent as it came in.

"What's it for, Genie? You only live once."

He shoved the flyers back into the binder. A heavyset old man sat opposite him, staring at a book through a huge magnifier. His bulbous nose, the eyes, gnarled hands looked familiar. A bubble of pleasure rose in Eugene's chest: He looked just like the old man in the fake Caravaggio.

Eugene pushed back his chair, carried the binder to the front desk, and asked the librarian if they had any books on Caravaggio. Without a flicker of surprise, she turned to her computer, and seconds later handed Eugene a number written on a PostIt note and pointed toward the reference section.

Library of Art. The volume was small, the cover picturing a fatuous boy leering over a bunch of grapes. Wondering if what he'd been drawn to wasn't attributable to Caravaggio but the "ceccio," whose name he'd forgotten, Eugene settled in an armchair by the window, and flipped past pictures of boys: boys playing musical instruments, boys eating fruit, a couple of girls, insipid as greeting cards. He kept turning pages. Toward the back, he found what he'd been looking for: scenes where something was at stake, one outside a temple, another in an arcade, a restaurant or pub, dramatic scenes, crowded with people, all lit with the same stage lighting. One image stopped him. A bunch of indifferent laborers were lashing an old man, certainly not Jesus, upside down to a slanting crucifix. The guy's domed forehead was ridged with pain, his neck and chest corded with anguish. Eugene could almost hear the dirty peasants grunt as they strained to hoist the cross, oblivious to the old man's pain. His torment, even his weight, was nothing to them. What did one old man matter?

Eugene closed the book. Rain beat against the window. The caption had read: "Crucifixion of St. Peter. Rome. Santa Maria del Popolo." Rome. He'd never been there. He imagined a dark church with incense and candles, with this painting behind an altar. A few people not needed elsewhere would be praying. He could sink into a pew, one of them, and be free to look as long as he liked. Afterwards, he would stroll down narrow streets, flower boxes, painted shutters, clotheslines. He imagined stopping at a splashing fountain, sitting at a cafe table in a linen suit, a little disheveled maybe, not exactly debonair, but with a few good years left. He ordered an espresso.

❖

"We encourage our clients to decorate their rooms with a few treasures from home."

Eugene had been led through the common areas of the Alden Arms Assisted Living and Extended Care Center by a woman whose name he'd missed, who was a dead-ringer for Shirley Booth with her floppy curls, cork-like nose, and permanent sad smile. She had shown him the swimming pool and hydro-therapy room, the atrium garden with burlap-shrouded shrubs that looked like standing corpses—"It's lovely once everything leafs out"—and now stood uneasily in a patient's room, taking in the Russian figurines on the window sill. The Venetian blinds were sandwiched between Thermopane. No cords to dangle. No rugs on the floor. This was the Memory Care floor.

"Safety, of course, is our main consideration," said Shirley Booth's look-alike. "We encourage personal items, but not furniture. That's out of the question."

"I thought we passed some rooms, on the other floor that—"

"Those are the suites. For couples, where both parties can function independently." She puckered her chin, commiserating, and ushered him into the hall. Eugene took a deep diaphragmatic breath, collecting himself; she pressed the elevator button. "We find the needs of our Alzheimer patients are best met in this especially designed wing supported by our especially trained staff."

They stepped into an elevator, deep enough to accommodate gurneys, and the doors shut behind them.

"It doesn't seem right to leave Glenna here on her own. You don't know her."

She turned to regard him and sighed. "Families are reluctant to let go, of course. But they don't realize how hard their expectations are on the confused individual. No one wants to disappoint, do we?"

Did she mean him or Glenna? Eugene wondered, as the doors opened on the lobby. She extended her hand. "I wouldn't wait too long. We have two openings right now, but they won't last."

❖

Eugene pushed aside their cereal bowls and reached across the kitchen table for Glenna's hands, bleached and weightless as winter oak leaves. If he squeezed, they would crumble. Instead, he touched his lips to their backs, first one, then the other. "Glenna, that audition I was telling you about, they've decided they want me. Can you believe that?"

She pinched her mouth, narrowing her eyes with suspicion. "It's disgusting."

"Why do you say that?"

She tugged her hands from his and began to keen. "Someone stole my picture of Momma. If they don't steal that alligator belt with the rhinestone . . ."

He put his hands behind her ears, his fingers slipping into her long silky strands, and drew her face toward him until their foreheads touched, hers so much cooler than his.

❖

Three orderlies hustled down the ramp of the Alden Arms as the cabbie deposited on the sidewalk a shopping bag and their two suitcases, hers old, his new. The two big fellows guided Glenna forward as the third reached for their bags.

"I'll take that one," Eugene said, pulling out the handle of the rolling suitcase he'd bought yesterday. "You get the others."

Glenna was already seated in front of the dark TV by the time Eugene got to her room. He tipped the orderly—from the surprised grin he realized this wasn't the custom—and unwound his scarf, afraid to look in Glenna's direction. From the shopping bag, he pulled her robe and hung it on a hook beside her coat. Glenna slid her feet back and forth on the linoleum, an irritating whisper.

"Glenna. Isn't it nice here? Everything fresh and clean." Keeping his back to her, he lined up pictures on the dresser, her as Serafina in *The Rose Tattoo*, Amanda Wingfield in *The Glass Menagerie*, Annie in *The Real Thing*. He stared at the shot of her in *The Gingerbread Lady*, unable to remember her character's name. A young female aide, black, walked in, carrying a folded walker.

"How 'bout a stroll?" When Glenna gave no sign she'd heard, the girl turned to Eugene, rattling the contraption. "Does she need this?"

He shook his head. "Where're you taking her?"

The girl propped the walker outside the door. "To the lounge."

"Can you wait a few minutes?" Eugene said. "I'd like to show you some of her things first."

Smoothing her smock, the girl sat beside Eugene when he unlatched the fastenings of Glenna's suitcase. Crowded inside were heaps of Glenna's old production stills mixed with headshots of famous actors, some she'd worked with, most she hadn't. Last week he'd bought them at Memory Lane Gifts: Gielgud, Bates, Richardson, Finney, Joe Mantegna, John Heard, an assortment of leading men. Sitting at their dining room table that was now on its way to the Salvation Army, he had signed each one, "Glenna, my dearest," "Glenna, you'll always have a place in my heart," and the like. "I'll never forget Marienbad," he'd written on the one of Alan Alda. "Always yours, darling Glenna" on Jeremy Irons. One by one he handed them to the girl, watching her cheeks round in pleasure as she recognized some of the faces.

"She used to be somebody, didn't she?"

Eugene looked at Glenna, hunched in the chair. "She still is."

The girl nodded, her beaded braids tinkling.

"I'm going to be gone for a while." Eugene quelled his rising dismay by willing himself into a character, a widower, retired from his job as a guard at the Art Institute, who'd taken three thousand five hundred dollars from his savings for his first trip to Italy. He was going to see all the Caravaggios in Rome. "While I'm away, could you take these out and show them to her? Talk about them. Now and then."

"Sure. We have a lot of nice clients, but nobody famous."

Eugene closed his eyes and saw Caravaggio's St. Peter with his left hand clenched around the nail impaling his palm. Right to the end, Peter was trying to pull himself free. He was alone. No one cared. No heavens opened above him. No angels waited to carry him off. There would be no divine intervention, this Caravaggio knew; that's how he painted Peter, refusing to give in.

Eugene stood, feeling dizzy, as if he weren't tethered by gravity. This was his last chance. He walked stage right to where Glenna sat, and bent low until his face was level with hers. Blood pulsed behind his forehead and pressed against his eyes.

"Glenna, I have a call back. They want me in Rome."

He could barely breathe. Through the blur, he focused on a horseshoe vein on her temple.

"Glenna . . . Glenna Glass, listen to me. When I go, this young lady is going to take you to meet some new people."

Glenna looked through him, threading and unthreading her fingers.

He fumbled with the handle of his unfamiliar suitcase, then walked unseeing into the corridor, his new shoes squeaking on the linoleum, walked into the blazing light.

"Call back?" he might have heard Glenna say, but he kept going.

Bird

OWEN WAS BURIED YESTERDAY. FROM the room next door, Boy's childhood bedroom, Martha hears Boy and his wife. Something something from Boy, then his wife, "Your mother can't manage. This house is falling apart. Your father let things go to hell around here, same as with the business . . ."

Patch's Hardware, three generations, is all Boy's now, and he can do as he pleases without Owen complaining.

Martha's been awake since the birds started their racket, thinking about what she read, how in India the dead are left on the top of towers for vultures to pick clean.

"She's got a bucket under the sink. I'm afraid to use the stove. Half the outlets—"

"Lower your voice. Mom'll hear." Then whispers.

Martha turns over. The wallpaper with sweet pea vines has yellowed. And the sheets stink. She can't remember when she last laundered them. Before Owen went into the emergency room the first time, two weeks ago. No, three. The smell of him must have faded by now, so it's just her. She smells like a washrag that's wiped up too many spills.

A suitcase wheels across the floor next door. From downstairs, there are noises in the kitchen. Everyone's leaving: Boy and his family back to their house across town, and Paul to Portland.

Martha pushes back the limp sheet and swings her feet to the ground. At her dresser, she looks at her favorite picture of her sons: Boy's around eleven, twelve; Paul, wearing too-big sunglasses, grins, accommodating Owen, the picture-taker. Boy refused to. Boy was the brave one. But Paul was the one who managed to get away. She sets down the picture and reaches for the pearls she wore yesterday, to the funeral. Gazing at her reflection in the mirror, she drapes the pearls over her collarbone, her speckled, saggy skin dissolving. Her throat is smooth and young, and Glenn is standing behind her, his tousled dark head nuzzling her neck as he slips off her bra strap. Young Martha reaches out to steady herself and touches the wall beside the mirror, touches the new wallpaper with the sweet pea pattern she'd hung recently, hoping to transform her marital bedroom into a romantic bower for her and Glenn. She had told Owen she hated the old stripes.

During the year she and Glenn were lovers, they'd been so careful. He'd never driven his own car, always borrowed one from his dealership's lot, parking a block or so away. But Sheryl Cardova, nosey bitch, had stopped Owen in their front yard one evening and asked if they were in the market for a new car, saying she'd seen Glenn Muncie, the Ford dealer, leave their house. Owen, who wasn't usually quick that way, guessed.

Glenn died of stomach cancer seven years ago.

Martha hears a cry, one of the grandkids. Bare feet running, kitchen chairs scraping, adults barking. Martha puts down her pearls.

Downstairs, in the foyer, Boy's wife restrains their two youngest, who're jabbering and pointing at something in the living room.

Boy is yanking a screen from the left window by the fireplace; one screen is already slanting over the coffee table where sits the tacky bouquet sent by the staff at the hardware. "To a great friend and boss. Forever in our thoughts." The florist's words, no doubt. Martha knows they resented Owen's meddling after Boy took over.

"What's going on?" Martha asks.

Both grandkids point. "It's a bird, Grandma."

It takes Martha a while to see what they're pointing at, a black blotch on the mantelpiece, next to the clock and the sympathy cards. A black rip is what it looks like. A hole. A perfect bird-shaped rupture in the logic of her living room.

Something moves. Not the bird. It's still as stone. It's the size of a grackle, but not a grackle, not shiny at all, but matte black, like a paper silhouette. It takes no notice of Boy waving the screen or Paul hurrying in with a broom; it takes no notice of Martha, or the grandkids yelping, or Boy's wife hissing, "Get behind it and swoop it out, out."

The bird remains unfazed. In all these years, there's never been a bird in the house. A couple of bats. No birds. What are the odds of this, a bird she's never seen the likes of, in the house the day after Owen was buried?

Paul jabs the broom like a bayonet. The grandkids scream.

"Wait," Martha says.

The bird swivels its head in her direction, takes a hop, and swirls into a whirling tourniquet of sooty energy, sucking at what's nearby, the sympathy cards, clock, candlesticks, the mirror above. Suddenly the spinning stops and becomes, again, the still black bird. It's looking at her, holding her with its pin-sharp eye.

Martha ignores Boy's question about his old butterfly net, and says to the bird, "What do you want?"

It dips its head cunningly and winks.

"Please God, no," she whispers. It's Owen come back.

"What, Mom?"

"Owen, no, you can't. It's not fair."

"Mom, it's not Dad."

Voices erupt.

"Paul, get that bird out of here!" "Did Grandma say it's Poppy?" "It is Poppy." "Don't hurt the bird, Uncle Paul."

Paul swings the broom, sympathy cards fly, children scream. The bird hops out of the broom's reach.

"Let me be," Martha cries.

Boy guides her to the kitchen.

After the bird is gone and Martha's drunk some orange juice, she says, "It's just stress. I haven't slept." When the screens have been replaced, the kids quieted, the house back in order, cars packed, and Martha has dressed, put on lipstick, and waved good-bye, promising to call them later, finally, they are gone.

From under the coffee table, she picks up a fallen sympathy card they'd missed. It's from Coral Muncie, Glenn's widow.

"In deep and understanding sympathy . . . "

The last time Martha saw Coral was at least a decade before Glenn died. It was at the garden center that has since folded. Martha had slipped out without saying a word.

Back then, Martha and Owen had been married for thirty-six years, thirty-four of them living in this house that Boy says is falling down. He's right. His wife is right. But where else does Martha have to go? This is the house of her marriage. Two sons, one miscarriage, three grandchildren, four parents buried, Owen's taking over the family hardware store from his father, business ups and downs, passing on the business to Boy, all this they shared. Only that one year with Glenn had she been happy, her private happiness.

Owen had walked into the kitchen where she was chopping stew meat and asked for Glenn Muncie's phone number. She lied, saying she didn't know, and kept her back to him as he dragged out the phone book.

He didn't bother to identify himself when he reached Glenn. "It ends now. It ends here. I won't tell Coral. I won't tell every goddamn person we know. I won't take this to Father. I won't take it to Ford Motor Company and whoever is your goddamn boss. I won't—" Owen stopped and listened to Glenn. "Right." Pause. Owen stood with his forehead pressed into the doorjamb, then straightened, saying, "For her benefit, and for my entire goddamn family's benefit." He listened again for what seemed like a long time. "That's it then. It's over." Gripping the phone, he turned it in Martha's direction, so both she and Glenn could hear. "It's over. He agrees. Nothing, do you hear, nothing happens now. No phone calls. No chance meetings. You see him on the street, at a party, you head in the other direction. You hear me." Owen was shouting now, and he kept shouting, but she heard nothing else as her life closed down.

A rock, Father Pat had said at the funeral. Their family was a rock.

Martha remembers so clearly Glenn's shock of black curls, the confident swing of his arms as he walked, the way his watch hung loose on his wrist, how his jaw moved when he concentrated, the whirl of hairs around his lip-pink nipples. She'd thought that all the molecules in her body had been re-aligned along an axis that was tilted permanently toward him.

After Glenn died, Muncie Motors became Stefano Ray Ford, and the farms that once surrounded the dealership were replaced by vast tracts of cheap houses. The town has gotten so big there are whole sections Martha's never driven through. If the Chamber of Commerce's sign is to be believed, the population's grown to nearly a quarter of a million. Glenn's house has changed hands three times that Martha knows of. It takes her a while to find Coral's current address.

Out in the county, Martha turns down a gravel road that winds past a Christmas tree farm, then peters out at a sun-baked lot with a small, neat ranch house, a flag pole, and a flourishing vegetable garden: corn, squash, beans on trellises, tomatoes, and a woman in a wide-brimmed hat, who stands to watch Martha pull into the driveway.

"Martha? That you? Come on in."

Martha is astonished that Coral's not surprised to see her. It's been almost twenty years. Coral's voice is the same, high and girlish, an affectation Martha had always thought, but she's gone skinny and odd looking, like some aging hippie in her tie-dyed tee shirt, overalls, and wild gray hair.

Coral peels off her gloves, drops each onto a tomato stake, two blue hands waving, and walks to her house, leading the way through cool, dark rooms into a bright kitchen. She flings her hat onto the open back door's knob, pours two mugs of coffee, and sets them on a small table.

"Take anything?"

"Just black," Martha says, uncertain, now, why she's come. She was curious, sure, curious to see what's become of Coral. It was to protect her that Glenn had heeded Owen and never called Martha again. If he had called, Martha would have left Owen, left her sons, left everything, but she has no intention of telling Coral any of this. After all these years, with both husbands gone, what would be the point? But Martha had thought she and Coral might share—what?—not exactly a bond, but something. The thought evaporates as she stares at Coral's freckled forearm while Coral doses her coffee with sugar and stirs until there can't be one un-dissolved crystal left.

Martha looks around the sunny kitchen: tea towel folded by the sink, a gleaming new faucet, a grocery list magneted to the fridge. Everything neat and snug. No broken tiles. No cabinet doors hanging crooked. No burn marks on the counter. Spotless. And nothing of Glenn. It was to find something of him that she'd come, she realizes. She wishes she could leave, but she's just sat down.

"I was sorry to miss the funeral," Coral says. "Owen was a good man."

"He was." Martha knows she should echo this cliché, say Glenn was too, but she can't bring herself to say his name to this woman. When he died, she hadn't sent Coral a card. Or flowers.

"He replaced all the rusted screens last spring." Coral nods to the window over the sink where fresh aluminum mesh sparkles with sunlight.

Screens? "That's nice," Martha says, wondering if Coral has a touch of what her grandkids call "old-timer's disease."

Coral gives Martha a look like she's missed something. "Owen, it was Owen helped me out."

"Owen?" This made no sense. Owen fixed Coral's screens?

"I thought that's why you came."

"I don't know anything about it." Martha's voice sounds false and tight to her own ears. "Owen didn't talk about work."

Coral's eyes widen as she stares at Martha. "Oh, dear Lord, no. It's not . . .

After I moved out here, what? Five years ago. I'd walk into the hardware with my list, leaky ice-maker, closet rod, whatever, and Owen'd ask if I knew how to do whatever—he could tell I didn't—and he'd offer to come out and see to it." A smile softens her face, remembering. "Sometimes he'd stay for lunch or a glass of iced tea. Never let me pay, of course. Never even let me give him anything from the garden. I told him he'd never make a go of the rent-a-husband business if he didn't take payment. Like I said, Owen was a good man. Nothing like Glenn, who'd chase anything in a skirt."

Martha can't breathe. "Glenn had affairs?"

Coral lifts her hands and presses the skin of her forehead, as if in the grip of a headache.

"Oh, Lordy, yes," she says. "Glenn, I'll give this to him, he was discreet. I only found out when the women started calling the house."

"Called your house?" Martha whispers. She had called him at the dealership.

"I guess they hoped I'd kick him out and he'd run to them."

"Why didn't you?" Martha squeezes her knees together. Women, Coral had said. Women. Plural.

"Kick him out?" Coral drops her hands and her face sags back. "Don't know. Over the years, I came up with different reasons. Excuses, really. Then I got sick, the cancer, then he got sick, and then it was over."

Martha stares at the coffee in her mug, its surface trembling from a vibration that comes from her. Women. She was one of many. She pushes back from the table.

"I'll get his things," Coral says.

"Things?" Something of Glenn's? Martha's face burns. Coral knows.

"Tools," Coral says. "Owen's tools."

"Tools? I have no need for tools."

"I thought that's why you came."

Martha can't tell if Coral's toying with her, or not. She stands, carries her untouched coffee to the sink, spilling some on her skirt, and hurries through the dark living room that Owen had been in many times. He'd been getting back at her; it didn't matter that she hadn't known.

"Let me at least give you some tomatoes." By the time Martha unlocks her car, Coral has sprinted to her side with a bag of tomatoes. "Take these."

Martha fumbles with her keys. By the time she starts the engine, Coral has set the bag in the back seat. Martha throws the car into reverse and hits the gas.

"Owen was a kind man," Coral calls out.

At the stop sign where the gravel road meets the paved, Martha pulls onto the shoulder, gets out, and lifts her face into the hot breeze. A red-winged blackbird she's disturbed swoops from a fencepost into the field. Owen wasn't kind—ask his sons—and he'd been a rock crushing her, but he was better at deception than she'd ever realized. For all this time. Had he been making amends for Martha? Or had he been cheating on her in a way that allowed him to pretend he wasn't really cheating? He and Coral might even have been lovers. Now he would never have to explain. He had escaped. But Martha hadn't. She had paid his price.

She reaches into the car for the sack of tomatoes. Standing fifteen feet or so from the stop sign, she takes aim and hurls a tomato at the rusted octagon, then another, waiting after each hit for a satisfying repercussion that doesn't come.

Lost and Found

"LAUREN, YOU MUST BE JOKING," Dallas said. "You can't let Frannie simply exit with no fanfare. We need something, her friends, me, and you, most of all. Good god, she's your mother. Nothing church-y, okay, but a wake is bare minimum essential."

Dallas, my mother's oldest, dearest, and gayest friend, was a force of nature, so three weeks later I waited at Frannie's condo on West 81st for him to arrive with the food trays. Dallas invited their co-workers from Holiday Heaven Travel Advisors, where Frannie had worked for twenty-some years, in the cubicle she shared with him, and I'd invited those whose names I found in her lizard address book: masseuse, personal trainer, dermatologist, podiatrist, manicurist, who was not the same as her pedicurist, whom I also invited, hair stylist, esthetician, etc. My roommate Constance and her current scowling, not-paying-his-share boyfriend begged off.

The guests were to arrive in a half hour.

I stood in front Frannie's gold-framed hall mirror. Where's the blonde hair that needs some fluffing? Those doll-blue eyes ringed with mascara? The too-bright pink lipstick that needs to be licked off those expensive veneered teeth? No more Frannie, mirror. You got me. Nice enough. Nothing special. Brown eyes. Brown hair, cut short, ends tucked behind my ears. No earrings. No makeup. "Like a goddamn Mennonite," as Frannie would say.

I put away her vacuum and placed the bronze urn with her ashes among the profusion of orchids by the one window that offered a sliver view of Central Park. The tacky urn would appall her. I was sorry about that. I was sorry this wake would seem humiliatingly inadequate to her. The Tavern on the Green would have been her choice. And I was sorry about the indignity of her death. Frannie had tripped down the stairs to the 59th Street/Columbus Circle subway station wearing four-inch-high, red patent leather, pointy-toed, sling-back Jimmy Choos. Broke her neck. She was fifty-two years old. "Forever young" was her theme song. What her vanity got her was a bunch of pervs looking up her skirt before the paramedics arrived. If she'd lived, that would have killed her.

On the plus side, Frannie would never grow old. On the minus side, I was alone in the world at thirty, an orphan.

Dad died of a brain aneurism/traffic accident on the Garden State Parkway when I was six. Mom sold our Colonial four square in Tenafly, bought this condo, went blonde, got her job at Holiday Heaven Travel, and insisted from then on that I call her Frannie. No more "Mom." Thanksgiving dinner at a Chinese joint and Christmas bingeing on old Meg Ryan movies with take-out, like "girlfriends." I had no living uncles, no aunts, and no cousins. "Who needs them," as Frannie would say.

Her doorbell rang and I let Dallas in. Even juggling the stack of boxed trays, he looked like an aging dress-shirt model, graying hair sleekly cut, cheeks rosy and burnished, as if he'd just enjoyed a hot shave with a straight-edged razor. Frannie gave me that detail, the straight-edged razor, implying that this should tell me a lot. I hadn't asked for clarification.

After we set out the trays, he handed me a glass of Prosecco, my choice, fewer bubbles than Champagne, more funereal, and said, "Maybe you could grab a scarf or a jacket from your mother's closet to dress up your outfit."

My "outfit" was a white shirt and black skirt. I thought I looked nice. "This is bad enough, Dallas, without you channeling Frannie."

"It doesn't matter. Everyone will think you're in mourning."

Then everyone will be wrong, I thought.

When the doorman called up, Dallas retreated to fuss over the buffet table, while I waited at the door to let in Frannie's friends, who arrived in packs of two and threes, mostly women.

"Terrible loss."

"If I can help in any way . . ."

"Such a nice apartment."

"She was one of a kind."

A blur of air kisses and moist hands gripping mine.

"This shouldn't have happened."

"I can't believe she's gone."

A fat man in a rumpled suit gave me his card. Fine leather goods, wholesale. A pregnant Indian woman held my hands and sing-songed something. I got away and refilled my glass.

"She was a lovely woman."

"And what great taste."

A grandmotherly woman patted my arm. "Death comes to us all, dear."

What was I supposed to say? "Thank you," I muttered, emptying my glass, then refilled it.

I searched the crowd for Dallas. He'd promised this wouldn't be hell. Standing by the orchids, nodding solemnly to a tiny woman in a green feathered hat, he glanced up and gave me an understanding look. But he didn't understand. Sure I loved my mother—you can't not love your mother—but not having to tug against her any more was a relief. Frannie wasn't the mother I wanted, and I wasn't the daughter she wanted.

Behind me I heard. "Frannie couldn't have been old enough to have a daughter in her—what—her twenties?"

I spun around, hugged the plump, disheveled woman with drawn-on eyebrows, and said, "Could you whisper that to her urn, about her not being old enough to have a daughter? She would be so flattered."

From the kitchen, Dallas smiled at me. I scowled back.

A woman with shiny red hair—a wig?—and a tipped-up pig's nose started telling me about her and Frannie's many shoe-shopping adventures. When she paused for air, I said, "Jimmy Choo killed my mother."

Her eyes panicked. Pleased, I walked away and found an open Prosecco bottle.

Someone touched my arm, a dweeb with a droopy eye. I wanted to throw up. Before he could speak, I said, "I've got to go," and ended up in Frannie's closet, sitting on a pile of shoes she hadn't bothered to return to their boxes, the shoes she must have tried on and rejected on the day she died. I picked up one silver high-heeled strappy sandal, a Dior. My head wobbled as I tugged off my black loafer and slipped the sandal on my foot. It pinched.

"These would be cute on you." Frannie had said. I was fifteen and we were in a discount store. My choice, I needed new gym shoes for PE. She'd thrust a purple furry boot at me, the kind prostitutes in Alaska probably wore. Jostled by bundled up women and hordes of kids, I glared at my elegant mother, who looked like a hologram beamed down from an elite and alien culture, and launched into an attack on Asian sweatshops providing unnecessary, junky shoes for the American market, breezing right past the hypocrisy of my wanting Nikes, which had been outed for their labor practices. "You don't think about what goes on anywhere else, do you, Frannie? You don't care about the consequences of your actions. You don't care about what's important. You're just a skeeter bug who skims along the surface—"

"Believe me, Lauren, on the surface is where you want to be. The murk that's below you need to avoid." She dropped the purple boot and stalked away. A little boy skipping past stopped to put the boot back where it belonged.

But even then, in high school, I knew that our fight wasn't just that I didn't want to be like her, the standard daughter/mother duel. By the time I moved out of the condo, when I was twenty-one, I sensed that a fissure existed inside her, an absence that made it impossible for her to connect with me, or anyone else. Dallas was her only close friend. He shared her love of light opera and designer sample shopping. Since I left home, he'd joined Frannie and me on our occasional Sunday brunches, making it possible for us not to quarrel. For this I was grateful.

I pulled off her silver sandal. Towers of Lucite shoeboxes surrounded me. This was her domain. Style was her diversion and a distraction from anything of substance. Her heart lived here. She loved clothes. Most of all she loved shoes. Kept them in perfect condition. Her feet, too. Twice monthly pedicures. I'd refused her invitations to join her. I picked up a gray suede pump. "Don't crush my Manolos," I heard her say.

Dallas found me crying and sent me home in a cab.

The next day, I returned to find Frannie's apartment cleaned, vacuumed, everything in place, trash bagged in the kitchen. "You're welcome," Dallas had scrawled on a doily propped next to her bronze urn. Was this addressed to me? Or to Frannie, for doing the best he could with her impossible—that was Frannie's favorite word for me—her impossible daughter?

I gathered the few things I wanted to keep: the shoebox of our family snapshots from before Dad died—we hadn't bothered to commemorate anything after that—his death certificate, my diplomas, the wallet-size photo of Frannie's much-older brother, Bobby, in his Army uniform, and the telegrams about his being shot down in Vietnam on January 15, 1972. He died when Frannie was twelve. In the yellowed picture Bobby looked like a boy version of my pretty mother, open face, high forehead, short nose, same vacant blue eyes, but already lost. She told me how he taught her to twiddle a penny back and forth between her toes, smoke Camels—unfiltered back then—and steer the car while sitting in his lap. I reminded her of this when I wanted her to teach me to drive, but she'd said, "Go to driving school."

Frannie's urn I left among the orchids by the window. I'd bury it next to Dad's, later, when I readied the apartment for the realtor. Her clothes and shoes I'd give to Thelma's Place, which supports a women's shelter in my neighborhood and where I buy most of what I wear. Carrying bags of family memorabilia, I returned to work at the copy center in Red Hook where I was the day manager. When I finished college, Frannie had urged me to get a "good" job, in Manhattan. "Why waste yourself in a dump serving the world's unwashed?" But I liked solving technical and mechanical problems, liked supervising the staff, and most of all, I liked the grateful customers, the kids with their lost cat pleas, the old women with their "found" notices, the Syrians, Koreans, Dominicans who came in with their hand-drawn, broken English, patched together layouts for flyers advertising their businesses, or menus, and I helped them re-work their pieces so they "looked American," as they said. I didn't charge for this, although the price sheet listed $25/hr for design services. I was salaried anyway. Frannie said I created better-looking litter. She nagged me about my job. She nagged me for living in a slum. She nagged me about how I dressed. She nagged me about everything.

Dallas was waiting in a window booth at the Olympic, the diner near Holiday Heaven. He wanted to give me Frannie's things from her desk at work. After our coffees and my cherry pie arrived, he slid over a lumpy envelope with Holiday Heaven's spinning globe logo. "They say you should get rid of your sex toys before you die."

"Please. I drew a curtain between me and any thought of Frannie's sex life." She'd had no boyfriends, which had always struck me as pathetic, given how much effort she put into her appearance. The lump turned out to be the clay ashtray I'd made in kindergarten.

"Curtain? You two had an entire drapery department between you."

"And that's over."

"Lauren, it's never over," he said, as I shook out what was left in the envelope. Frannie's work ID, and a heap of postcards, sent before smartphone photos killed postcards. Mali, Tierra del Fuego, Ivory Coast, Bhutan, Indonesia, Bangkok, absurdly pretty paradises now transformed into war zones. I picked up a card showing a thatched hut in front of a perfect turquoise sea. Dar es Salaam, postmarked 1999. Teddy + Mindy thanked my mother for her "AMAZING insights and X-treme helpfulness."

I handed it to Dallas, and he smiled. "Your mother was good at her work. She knew how to take care of people."

"Strangers."

"Not just strangers." His fork hovered over my uneaten pie.

I nodded for him to dig in, then I rifled through the heap of cards. One from Bangkok featuring a gold temple was addressed to Fran-ster— Fran-ster?—and sent to our home in Tenafly, not to Holiday Heaven.

Dear Fran-ster,

I fell down a rathole and found myself in paradise. All giggles and boom boom.

Come see.

Your loving bro,

The Bob-ster.

The Bob-ster? My Uncle Bobby? 12/10/87 said the postmark, which meant he was alive when I was three years old. But Mom, Mom and Dad, always said he was MIA. I flipped through the pile of cards again, and found one addressed to Fran-ster at our condo on 81st Street. Postmarked ?/?/98. I was living there then. I was seventeen. "Sawaddee from Bangkok" looped across a lurid sunset.

Fran-ster, My savior and angel and one true.

Thanx squared to the nth. $$$ arrived. Deal Sealed.

Come to Bangkok to visit your brother the Kapitalist.

Uncle Bobby was living in Bangkok, and my mom, who was as deep and deceptive as a Hostess Twinkie, never mentioned this to me. Could he still be there? The earlier postcard had been sent when Dad was alive. Had Frannie kept this fact from him, too? After Dad died, Ms. Twinkie sent money to her brother, but she hadn't gone to Bangkok. That I knew.

I re-read the message, trying to find some clue that would explain why she would hide her brother's existence.

Dallas reached for the card, but I held tight. "Did you know Frannie had a brother living in Bangkok?" A deserter? But this was hardly a reason to keep his existence a secret from me, her daughter.

"Lauren, we didn't talk family, except about you."

He took the card, and then squeezed my trembling hand. I pulled away. "Do you think this is an address?" I pointed to the blurred writing around the card's edge. Frannie hadn't cared that I might want to know my one uncle, even if he was a deserter. Wasn't that practically a badge of honor in that war? She didn't want a family, so she couldn't imagine that I might feel differently. She was that selfish.

"If you want, I can ask a Thai fellow I know."

"Do you think Frannie's brother could be alive?"

"Contact the Army and find out."

On the Vietnam War POW/MIA list, under Pennsylvania, I found Harmon, Robert J. under "Unaccounted for." 1978/01/15 Status: XX, "Presumptive Finding of Death."

Dallas' friend said the blurred writing on the postcard was an address.

I had an uncle. That he was alive mattered. That Frannie hid this from me mattered, too. She shouldn't have kept this secret. She'd left behind a few thousand in her checking account. I'd spend her money finding him.

In the time it took me to locate my passport, Dallas had arranged my cut-rate flight to Bangkok and booked me a comped hotel. I had plenty of un-used vacation time. His web sleuthing had produced the name of a shop at the address on the postcard, Uncle Bunny's—Uncle Bobby's?—T-Top Nails—the satellite picture of the neighborhood looked like a maze—

and a phone number I didn't call. Time zone, language problems, and what would I say to whoever answered the phone? Uncle Bunny, are you my Uncle Bob? Was there a real Uncle Bunny, or might this mean something in Thai? Maybe my uncle had no connection to the nail salon, but lived above it. Or had. He would be around sixty-four now, maybe long gone, or dead. There were too many things I didn't know how to ask on the phone. I wanted to see for myself. I wanted to go. Part of the reason, maybe the biggest reason, was that the journey, and even the distance traveled, would be an affront to Frannie.

Dallas warned me that Bangkok looked like Singapore but smelled like Ho Chi Minh City, which I figured meant like Bensonhurst, east of my Brooklyn neighborhood. The smell of rot cut right through the taxi's AC on the ride from the airport, and the squalor was way beyond the picturesque dilapidation shown in the Internet videos. When we entered an area of high-rises and glittering shops, Hermes, Mikimoto, Prada, the passing scene looked like a theatrical scrim. Nothing seemed real except the heat and the damp stench that clung to my skin. The cab stopped in front of a glass and marble hotel. I checked in, grateful the diffident man behind the desk spoke some English. I slept for a day and a half.

The doorman hailed a cab. Nervous, I handed the driver the address Dallas's friend had written in Thai and we nosed into a slow-moving stream of motorcycles and honking cars. Gold foil Buddhas swayed along the top edge of the windshield. I pressed my spine into the hard seat, trying to hold myself together. Fancy shops, palm trees, outdoor cafes, sunlight sparking off everything. I'd forgotten my sunglasses. After fifteen minutes of lurch-and-go, the cab darted onto a narrow street, and a few turns later, we entered a neighborhood of rundown two- and three-story buildings. I couldn't tell which direction we were headed. A skinny man tried to cross in front of the cab, but we raced on as the guy pounded the trunk. How was I going to find my way back to the hotel? I had its business card, but what if no one would help me? What if I couldn't find a taxi? What if I got mugged? If Frannie hadn't been secretive about having a deserter brother, I wouldn't have had to come. All this was her fault. One narrow street twisted into another and another. Short, wiry people hurried along the sidewalks. Flimsy stalls selling iAccessories, scarves, sundresses, umbrellas. Beautifully arranged, brightly colored fruits, each as enticing as Snow White's poison apple. After nearly colliding with a metal drum cooker and a man waving tongs, the cab pulled around a corner and screeched to a stop.

Through the swinging Buddhas, I saw a sign, hand-painted, red on yellow, in English and Thai, Uncle Bunny's T-Top Nails. Maybe the address written on the postcard was someone else's address, written like you might write a phone number on a dollar bill. I loosened my grip on the doily-covered headrest in front of me. Frannie's brother wouldn't have written someone else's address on a postcard inviting her to visit. An out-of-the-way nail salon might have been the best an American deserter could do. But wouldn't he have found something better by now?

Two old Thai women walked arm-in-arm past the salon's glass front.

Getting out, I stumbled over a little boy squatting on the sidewalk and apologized, which made him wail. I pretended nothing had happened and glanced across the lane at Uncle Bunny's. A narrow, one-story building with laundry lines on the flat roof. No second story where my uncle might have lived. I turned away, and faced a wall of chrome hubcaps for sale.

Short people flowed around me. In the hubcaps' distorted reflections, a woman in pink shorts now leaned against the doorframe of Uncle Bunny's. She flicked her long black hair and stared in my direction. I was a head taller than everyone else. Godzilla. I pushed into the crowd to get away. When I reached the corner, I stopped. The woman in pink shorts was gone. I turned and walked back.

The air conditioner above the door to Uncle Bunny's dripped on my shoulder. Inside it was so dark I could barely see, but I could make out a jar of lucky bamboo on a waist-high counter a few feet in front of me, and below, a red altar with a bowl of rice, like in every Thai restaurant in America. Twang-y music, maybe a cover of a Beatles' tune, droned. The air smelled of acetone and fake floral. To my right were two pedicure chairs, like those I'd seen through the window of Eeny Meeny's at the corner of my block. I'd never had a manicure or pedicure. At the closest pedicure chair, the woman in pink shorts bent over the feet of a squat woman with matted black hair and arthritic knees, who stared at me.

Behind the angled counter an old man watched me. I flinched. My uncle? Shaved, knobby head, face like a carved walnut, eyes cut into folds. He didn't look white, exactly, but maybe, or maybe Indonesian or Indian. Soft flesh, very tan, bulged between his wife-beater T-shirt and the waistband of his loose white shorts. His splayed legs were bony. Grimy flip-flops. Potbelly, skinny legs: a drunk's body, as Frannie would have said.

"You want mani/pedi?" His voice was honeyed and soft, not harsh Thai, not American, more Indian.

All I could get out was, "Just a pedi," pointing to my feet.

He slow-blinked toward the empty lounger.

I took off my flats, eased into the empty chair, and then set my bare feet in the attached tub that I guessed would be filled with water. He seemed smaller than I'd imagined Bob, but he slouched, so it was hard to tell. But he couldn't be my uncle. He was too foreign. In a few minutes I would ask if he knew him, when I wasn't so jangled.

From where I sat, he was partly hidden behind the angled counter, so all I could see of him was his head and narrow shoulders. He looked nothing like the boy whose picture was in my purse, not even adding forty plus hard years. And nothing like Frannie. Through half-closed eyes, he watched me. He could be anywhere between forty and eighty years old. To avoid his creepy gaze, I studied the photographs on the shop's back wall: five rows of eight by tens, close-ups of feet, some fat, some thin, some adorned with coy ankle bracelets, all with gaudy nails, but nothing fancy like the tiny cartoon characters, or the plaids and stripes, or the American flags displayed in Eeny Meeny's window.

Above the man were shelves of nail polish. I probably should have selected one.

I shoved my feet into my flats, then shuffled, with my right heel caught sideways, across to the shelves of nail polish above the man's head. Behind his ear a scar shaped like a question mark puckered his shaved scalp. I hated having to reach over him, hated my arm stretching out of the short sleeve of my blouse, hated the curve of my armpit exposed, was shamed by the warmth of my body radiating from me to him. I grabbed a bottle and I stepped back, almost tripping out of my folded-over shoe.

His eyes, obscured in shadow, swiveled in my direction.

I clutched the nail polish bottle so tight its cap cut into my palm, and croaked, "Do you know a Bob Harmon, an American?"

His expression didn't change. "He used to live here," I said. No response. "That was a while ago. Fifteen or so years ago." Nothing. Maybe the extent of his English was "mani/pedi." I continued. "Do you own this shop? Have you been here long?" He stared at me, no change. "An American," I repeated.

"You want pedi, you sit."

Was he smirking? I shuffled back and dropped into the pedi-chair, my pulse jumping under my skin. Could he see that I was shaking? I tried to focus on the tinny pop song.

Pink Shorts stood, flipped her hair over her shoulder, and arranged a small fan to blow on the finished toenails of the other customer. The old man mumbled something and the two women laughed. About me?

The whining pop song soared and I wanted to cry, like a stupid child. I didn't speak the language. I didn't understand one goddamn thing about where I was, in a dingy nail salon in a seedy section of Bangkok, half a world away from where I belonged. The creepy old man was useless. No one lived above this shop—and why would my mother's brother own a nail salon, anyway? This place had probably been a mail drop twenty years ago. There was a reason Dallas hadn't found other postcards from my uncle. He didn't want to be found, or he was dead.

Pink Shorts dumped water from a bucket on my feet, and sat to splash the warm water on my shins. Where she'd positioned her stool off to the side would give the old man a good view of me and my parted legs, if his eyes weren't closed. I pushed my skirt down over my knees, its back edge dipping into the water, and pulled the cloth tight. I was stuck here until this was over.

The other customer fumbled with her purse, dropped money in a tray on the counter, and was gone. The song changed, the AC wheezed. Something changed, something subtle. Even with the tinny music and the swishing water, a quiet had descended. Wishing I were any place but here, I kept my eyes locked on the jagged part in the sleek black hair of Pink

Shorts as she bent over my feet, trimming my toenails and pumicing my heels. The man's breath caught, a snagged wet rasp, as she set my feet, one by one, on a small cushion on the edge of the tub. While she massaged lotion into my feet, I felt his gaze slither over me. I looked up. His eyes were closed.

Sitting behind the counter in the dim light, he looked like no one I could imagine knowing. He wasn't my uncle. He couldn't be. And I hadn't even come to find my lost uncle. I didn't care about someone who'd never been a part of my life, or my family. I'd come to rebel against Frannie one more time, and spend her money doing it. That's what brought me here. Defiance, pure, simple, and stupid.

Pink Shorts continued to rub my feet. The creep's lips began to tremble, his eyebrows lifting when her fingers twisted between my toes. His eyes seemed shut, but he sensed or could hear her movements. Her smeary hands grasped my ankle. When her long fingers slipped slowly back and forth over my heel, along my arch and over my toes, he began to sway. His jaw thrust forward, the cords on his neck pulsing, and his breath came in gasps. He was masturbating. Behind the counter, he was masturbating. Inside me everything recoiled, but I sat rigid, unable to move. The woman's hands held me in place as she stroked my foot. Her grip moved to the other one, and she began again. Around me I dropped an imaginary glass wall. I could hear nothing, see nothing, feel nothing. I was in Frannie's closet, sitting on her shoes and around me floated her smell: the lily and clove of her perfume, Ivory soap, and the tang of foot sweat on leather. I could see her black stilettos, like two gleaming weapons, metal tips on four-inch dagger-heels, the arch a perfect handgrip. With shoes like these a woman couldn't run, but she could wound. She could gouge a creep's eyes until blood ran down the disgusting folds of his cheeks and dripped onto his hollow chest. She could do that.

Pink Shorts slapped my foot and placed it on the cushion. The perv whimpered, turning his face towards the windows. Light flashed from outside on the street, something moving. He lifted his eyebrows, his eyes opening wide, and, caught in the light, they were blue, the same color as Frannie's. Behind my collarbone, fragments blew apart, shards in a void, clicking and spinning, twisting, flying upward, falling. I couldn't breathe. My mother's brother. Wind whipped my face. I was in a car, windows down, in the driver's seat, roaring down a country road. Not me, a little blond girl with bangs and pigtails, sitting on her teenage brother's lap, his big hands beside hers on the steering wheel. She's laughing. Then she's not laughing. Her brother's hands are beneath her skirt, between her legs. Her eyes cloud. What can she do but hold on?

She had done her best. She had married Dad, built our safe, conventional life, and sent this asshole money to prevent him from ever coming back. She'd kept him a world away, from her and from me. She'd done this for me.

Something moved in front of me: Pink Shorts reaching for the polish bottle I held. I shoved her hand away, struggled out of the chair, forced my feet into my shoes, jamming my little toe, and walked toward the perv, stopping at the counter.

He lifted his chin to stare at me through slit eyes. "You look familiar."

"I'm no one you know."

From my purse, I dug out the Army portrait. I stared at that lying, innocent face, tore it in half, and dropped the pieces in the tray beside the other customer's cash.

I'm sorry, Mom, I am so sorry.

Outside, clouds blocked the sun, but no rain fell. Someone bumped me. I was caught in a crowd of people carrying folded umbrellas in preparation for what was to come.

Safe

FROM OVERHEAD KAREN HEARD BEN shut his bedroom door and cross the hall to the stairs. She straightened a flower that had drooped in the jug she'd set on the dinner table for his last night. He had arrived from Columbus where his dad, her ex, lived. He said he was on his way across the country to visit every place where he'd fucked up. His dad's, the psych ward in Indianapolis, she was stop number three. How many stops lay ahead, she didn't know. He had made a mess of his life in so many places. Her mother in Redwing was on his list, that much Ben had told her. Until he'd rumbled up her driveway on his motorcycle, she hadn't seen her son in eight years.

Steak, mac-and-cheese, she'd made his childhood favorites. Nothing green. He hated veggies. And no beer, but iced tea. On the phone, he said that he was sober, had been for six months. This seemed true. His eyes were clear; he acted remote, but not evasive. Most of the forty-eight hours he'd been here, he'd been out.

"Mom." He stood under the archway, eyeing the flowers. "You've gone to too much trouble."

Above his white T-shirt, which she'd laundered a few hours ago when he was out, the harsh planes of his wind-burnt face looked almost Indian.

When he arrived two days ago, she'd doubted she would recognize him on the street, and his gauntness still shocked her. The raging teenager she'd sent away had been big, broad as a refrigerator. That boy had dyed his thick blond hair black and shaved the sides of his skull. What he had now was stone-colored stubble.

"Nothing is too much trouble," she said. When she first saw him, she hadn't known what to say to him, and she still didn't. Everything, except small talk, threatened to lead back to the pain that had nearly annihilated her, and possibly him, too.

"Slice the steak, okay?" She pictured a knife in his hand and pushed aside a spasm of alarm. "I grilled it, and it's been sitting on the counter for fifteen minutes, doing whatever steak is supposed to do."

He suppressed a smile. She understood that he was amused at her aversion to handling meat. It pleased her to have given him this way to feel superior to her.

As soon as he was out of sight, she brought out the gift she'd wrapped in a big plastic bag printed with balloons, a leftover from the days when he took unwieldy gifts to other little boys' birthday parties.

"What's this?"

She jumped.

"A present," she said, nervous. Yellow? Balloons? He was twenty-six years old.

He set the steak platter on the table. "You shouldn't have."

Every sentence they spoke to each other was a cliché. She said, "Why not? Go on. Pull the tie."

The sack crumpled open, revealing a Darth Vader-like motorcycle helmet that she'd positioned on top of a folded, black, ballistic nylon jacket.

"Mom, you spent too much."

"What do you know?" She had spent too much. The pair together had cost over six hundred dollars. The squeaky brakes on her ten-year-old car would wait. "Just try them on. I want to see how you look."

As he slipped his arms into the jacket, his face softened, his first real smile. The tight knot behind her collarbone eased.

"The man said it has these hard plates, like from the space shuttle, in the sleeves and along the back to protect you if you hit the ground." She was talking too fast. She reached for the plastic sack and folded it, afraid to look directly at him, afraid to see his smile fade. "But you can take them out, if you want. And the fabric is extra-tough, to hold up to skidding across asphalt. Not that you will."

Ben shook his head. Foolish mother. "You don't have to worry." He zipped the jacket, which fit snuggly, then reached for the helmet, pressed it onto his head, smoothed the front of the jacket with both hands, then struck a pose, arms akimbo. Sheathed in black, towering above her, with his face hidden behind the reflective visor, he looked fierce and from a different species.

She locked her eyes on the large-knuckled hands jammed onto his hips. A man's hands, her son's hands, Ben's hands, not an alien's. "I should have bought gloves, too."

He reached for her. She stiffened and fought panic as he drew her into an awkward embrace. Her forehead knocked against the bottom of the helmet. He said something she couldn't understand.

She pulled back. "I can't hear you through that helmet."

He twisted it off. "Thank you, Mom."

She said what she had said to him twenty years ago when he was six and she'd made him wear a helmet with his little scooter: "I want you to be safe."

"I know." He set the black helmet on the table and unzipped the jacket. "Let's eat."

When he hurled the hot coffee pot at her—he was twelve—she'd believed that her golden boy had been taken over by a body snatcher. She'd wailed and he'd glared at her without recognition or remorse. She had reached out to him with her pink, scalded arm, but she couldn't touch him. Not then, not after her trip to the hospital, not in the weeks and years that followed. His teachers couldn't, his dad couldn't, nor the therapists, or the shrinks, not the whole team at that special school in Montana that he'd run away from, twice.

"It's no longer safe for Ben to live with you."

Was Dr. Willis saying that he thought she might hurt Ben?

She picked up one of the hacky sacks Dr. Willis kept for the teenage boys who were his specialty and put it back in the pile on the low table that she guessed was supposed to create a comfort zone between his shrink chair and the patient, or parent-of-patient, couch.

"Aren't lots of boys full of rage?" Threatening teachers, picking fights in the halls, breaking a kid's hand against a locker. Bad, yes, but couldn't this be the extreme edge of what boys did? The effects of divorce, distant dad, surging hormones?

"There has been an escalation. Ben has spoken of wanting to kill you."

"I know he says he hates me, like when I tell him he can't do something or he has to quit watching TV and do his homework or. . ." She fixed her eyes on the ugly abstract watercolor behind Dr. Willis's head. "Isn't it normal to say you hate your mother? I know I did, when I was a teenager."

Dr. Willis nodded slowly. "Saying you hate, that's common. Threats, that's less common. But we worry when the thoughts move into planning and when the planning becomes specific."

"Specific?"

"He has thoughts of sneaking into your bedroom at night while you sleep and stabbing you with a kitchen knife."

After that last school in Montana, Ben disappeared.

The Ben who had roared into her driveway a couple of days ago was a stranger. There. Another cliché. The forceps scar above his left eye was the only familiar thing about him, yet being with him, having him here, made her giddy as she veered between happiness and wariness, uncertainty and hope. She wanted Ben back.

She brought in the mac-and-cheese and reached over him to set down the casserole, startled again by how thin he was. Did he see any changes in her? He hadn't noticed, or at least hadn't mentioned, that she'd cut her long brown hair and dyed it blonde to cover the gray. He hadn't noticed, or at least hadn't mentioned, that she'd replaced most of the furniture with a few spare modern pieces. He hadn't noticed, or at least hadn't mentioned, that the only room that remained unchanged was his bedroom. He hadn't asked about her job or her life. He hadn't asked what she'd been up to in the past eight years. Hadn't asked if she had a man in her life. Children aren't interested in their parents, her mother had said last night when Karen called her to talk about Ben when he was out. Most of the time he'd been here, he'd been out with friends from childhood. She'd been surprised he'd stayed in touch with them, and wounded. Before his call last week, he hadn't phoned her or sent a postcard in eight years.

He piled steak and mac-and-cheese on his plate and began to eat before she'd unfolded her napkin. Maybe he'd picked up lousy manners at that school in Montana, or maybe he'd been in prison. She wouldn't ask. She didn't want to risk offending him; she didn't want him storming out. As he forked up his food, she asked whom he'd seen that day.

He'd met up with Denny, who now sold real estate; Marcus—Karen saw Marcus often at the restaurant he managed for his father; and Beck, who was the golf pro at the country club. Beck was now thinking of going back to school.

"In what?" she asked. Beck had been a stoner, but he'd managed to finish high school. Ben hadn't.

"Business," Ben answered, his mouth full.

"Do you ever think about going back to school?"

He leaned back in his chair, and shook his head. "I don't see the point."

Karen tried not to take this as a rebuke. She taught English at the high school and ESL at the community college.

"Come fall, I'll figure out the next step," he said. "I've got a buddy who has a small farm outside Joplin. He said he could use some help. I'll see."

A buddy in Missouri? A friend she'd never heard of from a life she knew nothing about. "Are you interested in farming?"

"I'll find out. It's only temporary. I don't have to settle down."

Had their life, her regular schoolteacher life, been too settled for him? If she'd been an adventurer, would that have been better?

"I forgot the iced tea," she said.

She opened the fridge and breathed in the cold air. Had everything she'd done been wrong?

"So where are you going next?" she asked, filling a glass for him and one for her.

"Up to the Boundary Waters. Camping. I've always wanted to go there."

"Remember Camp Ryder?" Which was in Minnesota. Ben had been eleven. He called home begging for money to buy extra bullets for target practice. She'd refused. His counselor called later to say that she'd done the right thing. He was worried about Ben.

"Near there, but beyond. Spend a week or so, then I'll go down to Grandma's."

"Have you called her yet?" She'd told her mother to expect a call.

"I'll take care of it." He hunched over his plate. End of conversation.

She picked at her food, trying to pretend his silence didn't hurt.

"I tried to take care of you," she said.

He exhaled a deep breath and set his knife and fork on his plate—he'd finished eating—then placed both hands on the table's edge, as if bracing himself, and looked directly at her. "You did the best you could, I want to say that. I was a hard kid, I really made it tough for you, but you did your best. I was lucky. I am lucky. Thank you."

Nothing in his expression suggested that he meant it, but she clung to his words waiting for them to make sense.

"I was lucky, too," she said. "Am lucky." Lying and not lying. Suddenly she was tired, weary from trying to reach across the gap that separated them. She wanted him gone, but she didn't want him to go.

He stood and bent to wrap his arms around her shoulders saying he had to get his things organized for tomorrow. She shooed away his offer to help in the kitchen, then listened to the floorboards in his room squeak. After tomorrow she might never see him again. At least she was sending him out on the road safe.

From the bottom of the staircase, she called up, "In the morning, I'll go out and get those buns from Nielson's that you like."

The sun woke her before six. She dressed, tiptoed past his room and, downstairs, peered through the dining room window. His motorcycle blocked her car. She would walk to Nielson's through the backyard and down the alley. Returning, she saw that his window shade was still lowered. She eased open the kitchen door, so as not to wake him, turned on the coffee pot, and shook the rolls onto a plate. On her way upstairs to say that it was time, she glanced out the dining room window and saw her car in the driveway, but not his motorcycle. Her heart clenched. He had left. He had left without saying good-bye. He was gone. She gripped the banister, afraid she might fall. Had he worried that she'd make a fuss? Ask when she'd see him again? Ask him to stay in touch? It was okay. She understood. This didn't mean that he wouldn't come back.

Or he might have just moved his bike when he strapped on his sleeping bag and duffle.

She hurried upstairs and tapped on his door. "Ben?" and slowly opened it. The clothes that had been scattered on the chair and floor were gone, along with his duffle. In the middle of his unmade bed sat the motorcycle jacket, folded neatly, with the black helmet on top.

Above his little boy neck and little boy shoulders his flame-colored helmet had been gigantic. To the corner of the block and back was as far as she would let him go. Helmeted head bobbing, body hunched, hands gripping the handlebar that billowed tassels, his right foot on the scooter, his left slapping the sidewalk, he raced away from her as fast as he could.

The Gold Spoon

"SWEETIE, THIS IS FOR YOU, from your uncle Virgil."

The girl took the tiny gold spoon. "Is it from heaven?"

"No, darlin'." Kitty hugged the girl into her lap. "It came. . .the Army sent it along with his other things."

The girl lifted the spoon into a band of light streaming through the Venetian blinds. "Was it from when he was little?"

"I don't believe so. He must have got it special for you."

"For my birthday." The girl lowered the spoon to sip from its bowl, pretending she could taste the light.

IT WAS HIGH SUMMER AND there'd been no rain for weeks, not since the shooting stopped three months ago and their division moved east into Land Salzburg. "Mountains but no breezes," Pfc. Virgil Griffin had written to his folks. "Hot, like Henderson, and dull." The truth and a lie.

Virgil had just returned to barracks when Knuckles, Sgt. Knuckles Sonofabitch Herwig, kicked his bunk. "Look lively, soldier."

Virgil lowered his worn copy of *Collier's*. And there was Knuckles' glad-hand sidekick, Clay Harnedy, too. A bad day had just gotten worse.

"Now, Okie." Knuckles kicked the bunk again.

That afternoon they'd caught a couple of German soldiers trying to pass as civilians, and found a baby, dead, in a suitcase. Virgil sat up and pulled on his boots. What he needed now was pictures of American housewives in their immaculate kitchens and freckle-faced kids chasing dogs. "Where're we going?" he said. Knuckles was already gone.

"To the Property Control Warehouse," Clay said, admiring his mustache in the pocket mirror taped to the empty bunk above Virgil. "Haul some crates out to the CO's."

Why me? Virgil didn't bother to ask.

Two Jeeps waited: one standard issue, the other with a reinforced windscreen, the kind that protected against the de-capitation wires the saboteurs had begun stringing across the roads.

The PC Warehouse was an old brick building, half a city block in size. Inside, two steps behind Knuckles and Clay, Virgil could barely see anything except a small lamp casting light on a desk, with a guard asleep, tipped back in the chair. Virgil propped his M1 against the wall, next to Knuckles' and Clay's, and a shot rang out. He dropped to a crouch. The guard jerked upright; Knuckles and Clay started laughing. The warehouse door had slammed shut. Heart pounding, feeling like a fool, Virgil slipped his revolver into his holster. Knuckles said something to the guard, who pushed away Knuckles' clipboard.

"Closed. Come back after eight hundred hours."

Knuckles hefted his hip onto the desk and leaned over the guy, shoving the clipboard under the lamp's beam. "Note the signature." He tapped the form. "And this here, where it says, 'to be delivered between twenty-two hundred and twenty-four hundred hours on 21 July to the residence of the Commanding Officer.' So, right here, below these instructions, write—what d'you think?—'refused access' and clearly print your name. Then we'll be on our way."

With no change of expression, the guard launched his rolling chair toward the wall behind him and tugged open an electrical box. Explosions like distant shots rang out—Virgil checked his reflex—and the overhead lights flickered on. Virgil could now see that the place was stacked floor to ceiling with barrels, crates, and overstuffed pasteboard boxes. This was where the Army stored what they confiscated from the Nazis. He counted the aisles: more than sixteen, to the right alone.

"We're going to need some handcarts," Knuckles said.

The guard nodded to the left where a collection of handcarts and dollies were parked in front of a shadowed metal cage packed with loot: paintings, statues, chandeliers hanging from hooks, and racks of furs. Knuckles snapped his fingers at Virgil. After wrestling free a couple of dollies, Virgil stuck his fingers through the mesh. Touching the sleeve of a honey-colored fur so downy he wasn't sure he'd touched anything, he remembered Charlotte's neck.

"I won't," she'd insisted, when he said she could date other guys while he was gone, and she'd arched her neck for him to kiss.

A sudden click, like a safety released. Virgil flinched and turned to see a flame leap from Clay's fist to the guard's face. The guy, smiling, leaned back and exhaled a long plume. A cigarette, a Zippo. Virgil unclenched his fingers—he was on base; he was safe; he had to quit over-reacting or he'd catch hell. He forced his legs to move, and grabbed the dollies.

Clay interrupted his story about a broad in Wiesbaden, and Knuckles pointed to the warehouse's floor plan, pressed under the desk's glass. "You get Lots 512a and 512aa and go careful. It's dishes. We'll get the rest." He settled his haunch onto the desk, going nowhere fast.

Virgil pushed his dolly down the second aisle, feeling Knuckles' eyes on him, then, at the first break, zigzagged into the next aisle. He'd heard that a train loaded with gold had been captured in Werfen a month ago, some forty-four cars, but all he could see were suitcases, trunks, ordinary people's things, and office stuff: desks, files cabinets, and crates.

Out of earshot of the others, he paused to look at a brass-studded steamer trunk plastered with stickers from fancy resorts: Lake Como, St. Moritz, Monte Carlo, and one with Zugspitze written across a perfect blue sky. Impossible to connect these ritzy spots with what he saw every day: the bombed-out landscape, haggard women, snuffling kids, the few men too old or damaged to be soldiers.

He wiggled the trunk forward, curious about the owner who'd holidayed at swanky resorts. Back home, he'd never been anywhere except the state capitol. Hangers inside jingled like chimes. He pried open the sprung lock and a musty tang floated toward him: a blend of dusting powder, perfume, and what he often smelled on the DPs, an odor both rotten and sweet. Silky dresses spilled out. Bending to pick them up, he touched something hard: a small leather box. Telling himself he shouldn't, he opened it. Inside was a gold chain with a Jewish star. In his first days here, he'd been sent out with a squad to search nearby farms for German soldiers in hiding. It was a hot day, no shade, all the trees burned for fuel the winter before. At the end of the morning, they came to a farm that was a ruin: no livestock, the house roofless, the outbuildings gutted. From what was left of the barn, they rousted a thin, big-boned woman. "Cow or *frau*?" someone joked, as they led her to the middle of the yard. She stood rigid, staring through the soldiers that ringed her. In spite of her ragged dress, she reminded Virgil of the statue on the lawn of the Henderson courthouse, the granite woman holding a wreath, the same wide brow, the same stern jaw. As his squad went through the house and the other outbuildings, kicking at doors and shouting, her stillness seemed to swell into an indictment. A little girl ran from behind a shed and grabbed her legs. Even then, the woman refused to shift her gaze. In the end, they found no German soldiers, only a few blankets, a bucket of turnips, and, miraculously, a fresh loaf of bread. When they drove away, he looked back. The girl had ducked behind the woman's skirt, but still the woman hadn't moved. "She might be Jewish. They can't tell the difference between us and the Nazis," the Captain had said. Virgil dropped the necklace with the Jewish star back in its box. The woman who'd worn this would never claim her trunk.

He found Lots 512a and 512aa and squatted to smoke a cigarette.

When he was in high school, the war was only a disturbance, like a long tornado season. Adults talked about it, and his teachers turned it into lessons with maps and colored pins. In his parents' apartment the radio was always on, the news reported by urgent voices with sirens sometimes in the background, but the menace was safely on the other side of the two oceans, a fight between foreigners. After America entered the war, he had studied the pictures in *Life*, envisioning himself belly-crawling up a hillside to pick off Krauts, and in his senior year that poster of Uncle Sam scowling "I want You for the U. S. Army" spoke directly to him. Was enrolling in the university and joining the ROTC in the fall, which was what his parents wanted, the honorable path? Or was it shirking? Kitty, his older sister, came home with baby Joanie, after her husband shipped out of San Diego, and they took over the second bedroom again, sending Virgil back to his childhood bedroom off the kitchen, making him feel even more useless. Without telling anyone, right after graduation he signed up, joining the 42nd Infantry Division. He made it to Europe four months before VE day. He had seen soldiers die. He had killed no one. After the surrender, the momentum gave way to confusion and fragmentation, sabotage and an endless river of refugees. The magazines his mother sent didn't have pictures of any of this.

He stood, stubbed out his cigarette, and maneuvered the two heavy crates onto the dolly. What did the CO want with confiscated dishes? When he got to the front desk, the guard was smoking, his feet on the desk, with Clay's lighter beside his boots.

"Do you need to check off these numbers?" Virgil asked.

"Taken care of." The soldier blew a smoke ring. Virgil picked up his M1, left beside the door—Clay's and Knuckles' were still there—and pushed his dolly outside.

Dusk was coming on. The Jeep with the windshield held a crate the size of a twin bed mattress, on which was stenciled a swastika and Szalasi, the name of Virgil's old gymnastics coach and, as he now knew, a town in Hungary, to the east. Mr. Szalasi had been universally hated. He had tormented Virgil, among others, and fawned over the jocks who dominated on the pommel horse, but seeing Mr. Szalasi's name here dismayed Virgil, as if something he counted on to maintain an essential separation between home and this hellhole had collapsed. Fighting the sensation that the ground was swaying, he leaned forward against the Jeep. Behind the driver's seat was a small wooden chest, the kind that held pistols.

The warehouse door banged open and a flatbed cart, pushed by Clay and piled with boxes, rumbled toward Virgil. Knuckles, carrying both of their rifles, followed.

"Lend Clay a hand, asshole," Knuckles said to Virgil, climbing in the driver's seat of the empty Jeep. "Then get your sorry ass over there. You're riding shotgun with him." He pointed to the other Jeep, with the big crate and the small chest.

When everything was loaded, Clay settled into the driver's seat, beside Virgil, and pulled out in front of Knuckles. The lead Jeep had to be the one with the safety windscreen. At the checkpoint, Clay turned off their headlights; they weren't allowed off base. Virgil hid his worry and kept his hand on his rifle. A sickle moon had risen, barely enough to see the potholes in what remained of the road. Clay drove slowly through block after block of ruins and rubble. No one was out—there was a civilian curfew—but a few cooking fires flickered among the ruins. Not talking made Virgil more nervous. He turned sideways to steady the big crate behind that jostling his shoulder. "What's this?"

"Hey," Clay shouted, swerving wildly: a tire in the road. Alarm corkscrewed through Virgil. A booby-trap? He fired at nothing. Knuckles' Jeep swung wide, too.

"Nice one, farm boy."

Virgil said nothing.

When they reached the outskirts of town, Clay began to hum, then broke off to ask, "Like music?"

"Not much."

"It's a harpsichord."

"What?"

"What's in that crate."

"Harpsichords have legs." Clay was conning him.

"Maybe these fold." Clay began to hum again.

"And in the chest? Pistols, right?"

"Aren't you the nosy one? Keep your eyes on the road."

The air was cooler once they reached the hills. The moon slipped behind a cloud, making it hard to see the way ahead. Clay slowed, cursing the darkness, but by now Virgil could see clearly. He could even see things he knew weren't there: a figure crouched beside a boulder, the glint of a gun barrel.

For officers' quarters, the Army had commandeered an enclave of houses on a lake that was surrounded by a forest, the only one left in the district. When the road entered a stretch of tall evergreens, Virgil knew they were close. Clay downshifted, and behind them, Knuckles' Jeep fell back. Virgil slouched behind the windscreen, not trusting the reinforcing, and imagining wires strung across the road from tree trunks on either side. The crate bounced against his shoulder.

"So why would the CO want a harpsichord?"

"To impress the locals, you jughead, along with this other shit."

"I'd think—"

"Think? Who gave you permission to think? Look for a turnoff to the right. There's supposed to be a sign." He slowed, and behind them, Knuckles downshifted too.

MPs were posted at the checkpoint. Clay showed their orders to a Yankee MP, who told them the CO's house was half a kilometer on. "Look for big urns."

Virgil kept his eyes forward. A harpsichord made no sense.

Pine branches met overhead. Clay inched along the rutted track. Through the trees, Virgil could just discern the shapes of big houses set far apart. Knuckles' Jeep hummed behind them. The urns appeared and Clay steered between them. Fifty yards on, trees framed what Virgil took to be the CO's house. The outlines of two windows on the first floor were visible where the blackout curtains failed to cover. Knuckles drove his Jeep alongside and said something to Clay that Virgil couldn't hear. Clay cut the engine and jumped out, saying to Virgil, "You stay here. We're going to deliver what's in Knuckles' Jeep first."

"Need me to help?"

"Stay here."

Why not drive both vehicles to the house? Virgil wondered, watching their Jeep creep forward. Why'd they bring him along anyway? Without him, they'd maneuvered the biggest crate out of the warehouse and into the Jeep; the two of them had the driving covered; and if it was so important to have someone ride shotgun, why not another grunt to ride with Knuckles, too?

At the CO's house, a door opened, silhouetting Clay against the light from inside. Virgil propped his M1 against the dashboard and climbed into the back. Wedged behind the "harpsichord," the small chest had bounced open and something beside it glittered on the grooved floor. He pried loose a tiny, gold spoon, no bigger than his thumb. A child's spoon. He'd never seen a gold spoon. He opened the chest whose lock had sprung. Nestled into fitted compartments were tiny spoons, forks, and knives with scalloped blades, all gold. Real gold, of that he was certain.

Not far away gravel spattered as the other Jeep approached. He slipped the spoon into his pocket.

"You want me to drive this up to the house now?" Virgil asked, climbing back into the front seat.

"We'll take care of it," Knuckles said. "We'll take it 'round back ourselves."

Virgil glanced over Knuckle's shoulder toward the dark house. "The crates with dishes go in the front door, but a harpsichord you're taking to the kitchen?"

"Yours not to reason why, asshole." Knuckles lumbered from the Jeep.

"You're going to drive this baby," he tapped the Jeep's wheel with his boot, "back to base."

The one without the windscreen? "I can wait," Virgil said.

"We'll be a while," Clay said. He jerked his head for Virgil to get down. "There's a couple of broads, a maid and the cook."

This was a lie. Some sap from the quartermaster would cook for the CO. Not a broad. "I'm in no hurry," Virgil said.

Knuckles smirked. "Adios."

"I'm not driving that Jeep back, alone, not without a windscreen."

Knuckles flexed his arms. "We're talking orders here, private," and Clay added, "We just drove that road. Nothin's there. Nothin'. You think it's been booby-trapped in the last few minutes?"

"Possibly." There was no sign of life at the CO's now, no faint glow from the back where the kitchen would be.

"Get going," Knuckles said.

Virgil stared at him. So this was why they'd corralled him: to drive back the empty Jeep. As soon as he drove off, they would drive whatever was in the big crate and the gold somewhere else to stash. The checkpoint's log would show he'd returned on time and later Knuckles would sneak the other Jeep in another way. He had contacts. Any trouble, Knuckles would insist a mistake had been made in the logs, and that the two vehicles had returned together. And Virgil was here because he was a shitass country boy who wouldn't catch on. If he let on that he had, they'd either offer him a piece of it—unlikely—or they'd kill him and blame it on the Germans. Knuckles would garrote him, right here. They'd dump him and the empty Jeep somewhere on the road and make it look like sabotage. Their late return would be explained by his "ambush."

"Is there a third maid?" Virgil said, pretending he'd fallen for it.

Knuckles pulled Virgil's M1 from the Jeep with the harpsichord and handed it to him. "Get going."

Careful not to rush, Virgil climbed in the empty Jeep, shifted out of neutral, and eased up on the hand brake. When he stepped on the foot feed, the gold spoon pressed against his thigh. The spoon was his proof. In the morning, he'd take it to the CO. If this fancy gold silverware had been requisitioned, fair and square, he'd be thanked for his caution, and that would be that. Or, the CO would send the MPs to arrest Knuckles and Clay.

Virgil saluted the sentry at the checkpoint, then kept to the middle of the road, navigating more by feel than sight, the air in his face. Only a few Jeeps had windscreens. Most of the time, no problem. But his plan had a flaw: snitches wound up dead. Hell, it could even be that Knuckles and Clay were working for the CO.

He glanced back, half-expecting to see the other Jeep with a rifle glinting in his direction, but everything was dark. Torn between his gut feeling that they were following him, and his certainty that they believed he was a stupid rube, he concentrated on the barely visible road, the spoon biting into his thigh. He should have left it where it was. His bowel contracted. What he needed was a cigarette. Not lifting his eyes from the road, he coaxed one from his shirt pocket and held it between his lips—anyone lying in wait would hear him before they saw a tiny red ember—but he didn't reach for his lighter. The weight of the cigarette on his lips made him think of a woman's lips parting, a red-tipped finger plucking a speck of tobacco from her tongue, not Charlotte, no one he'd know in Henderson or ever seen, but the promise of a woman he would meet someday and take to fancy resorts, in the life he was meant to live.

He glanced over his shoulder. No sign of anyone. He touched the spoon's outline. He wouldn't take it to the CO, because getting back at Knuckles and Clay wasn't important. Getting out alive was.

The wind stopped. He heard a dove cry. At exactly the moment when he realized it was early for a mourning dove, a sound like a rising ocean slammed past him, leaving in its widening trail a vacuum of silence. His eardrums trembled. From the outer membrane of the ballooning silence came a whistle. And something stung his forehead. Before the fingers of his right hand could ease their grip on the wheel to swat away—what? a moth? a mosquito?—both hands ripped loose and he was flung backward. The moon directly above pulled free from the clouds and raced toward him while he flew up toward it. And far away, behind him, his foot hit the emergency brake, and his hip smashed against the Jeep's frame. Dark branches beat around him. In that arched trajectory, his neck snapped so loud the reverberation boomeranged away, stalled, and then rushed back toward him, not as sound but light. Firecrackers crisscrossed the sky. A light-filled box cracked open, and people streamed out and flowed past him, soldiers in flak gear, DPs, his gym coach, Charlotte beaming, his parents, the corporal who'd died that first night, his sister and little Joanie, Knuckles and Clay, others, so many that he knew but couldn't name, until the light from which they came swelled to the ends of the sky and took him in.

A Little 1-2-3

"COMING TO LUNCH?"

Annoyed at the interruption, Betty glanced toward the door. Today it was Sylvie, chief of the "you've got to stay involved" do-gooders who refused to leave her be. Betty clicked off the TV—among the few pleasures left were her morning shows—and pushed out of her rocker. Protesting did no good. No one listened anyway, not the decrepit fools she had to live with, not the Nurse Ratchets, not her son Jack who'd said, "It's only temporary," when he moved her here.

Betty followed Sylvie down the glass-walled corridor toward the dining room, dismayed to see that the snow had retreated to a ragged line under the shrubs along the nursing wing. All winter, inside the glare and incubator level heat maintained by The Courtyard Assisted Living Center, she'd looked out at the wind-scoured land and the leaden sky and found it fitting, just exactly how the world should look now that Loyle was gone. She tapped on the window—the sun had no right to sparkle on the tawny grass—and remembered watching the stars with Loyle, wrapped in blankets, inhaling the damp, leaf-sweet smell of dirt, and him saying, "Can't you hear the bloodroot and ferns uncoil?"

Sylvie tugged at her skirt.

The dining room's glass doors swung open. Since breakfast, the staff had gotten busy with pots of fake flowers and cardboard cutouts of Easter baskets. Like a goddamn kindergarten. Sylvie led the way to their table where the regulars were already seated: the Urso sisters; Muriel Schneberger, who drooled; Caroline Meister; Harold Rasmussen, a new guy with a hand problem who never talked; and Tony Vito, who thought he was God's gift. Avoiding Tony, Betty took her chair next to Harold. Sunlight poured through the long stretch of windows, drenching everything in yellow.

Tony's rasping voice cut into her reverie. "That's what cataracts do."

Betty looked at him and was shaken by his sassy grin. Had she spoken out loud? She covered her confusion by putting a roll on Harold's plate and wrestling with his Smart Choice packet as one of the women said to Tony, "Must you always look on the ugly side?"

"What other side is there? Got to know what you're dealing with." He twisted one of the fake daffodils in the centerpiece.

"Don't fiddle with that," Sylvie snapped.

Betty pretended she was sitting at her own kitchen table, with Loyle. He looked up from his coffee mug and said something she couldn't hear. She reached for his hand and heard a guffaw. She blinked. Tony Vito leered at her. Both Ursos were smiling.

"What is it?" Betty demanded, her face prickling.

"It's okay, dear," said Sylvie, smiling her know-it-all smile. The others bobbed their heads.

Alarmed, Betty looked down and saw her hand laced in Harold's, not Loyle's. She jerked away.

"It's springtime in Eau Claire and the birds and bees are humming," Tony sang.

"You're a jackass, Tony Vito." She glared at him. "If my husband were here–"

"But he isn't, darling. He checked out."

"Ascended to heaven," added Lily Urso.

"Not old Loyle," Tony said.

"Tony, why don't you–" Sylvie interjected.

"It was an accident," Betty hissed, the air squeezed from her lungs.

"Accident, schmaccident." Tony pointed his finger at his temple and fired.

Betty swatted the paper daffodils in Tony's direction. "He was cleaning his guns."

Tony straightened the overturned pot. "You're telling yourself a fairy tale, sweetie."

Sylvie slapped the table. "Stop this now." The water glasses shook.

Betty forced back her chair and rushed from the table. An aide got to her before she reached the door.

She didn't argue about the pill.

Drifting in and out of sleep, she saw Loyle's head beside her, turned away, his silky white hair curling over his creased neck. Below the covers, she touched his back where his skin sagged over his shoulder blades, loose and white, speckled with moles. They never wore nightclothes, not even in the coldest weather. "Climb on top of me and I'll be your furnace." She turned to her side, rotating her leg to rest where his thigh should be. "I can take old age," she'd told him, "but I can't stand that you might die before me." He'd laughed and said it wouldn't happen.

"Promise me."

But he'd broken his promise. From the door, she heard whispering. Sylvie.

"Leave me alone," Betty called out.

"I told Tony he can't sit at our table any more."

Betty kept the blanket over her head until the door closed.

Loyle tossed his final wages on the kitchen table, saying Patel didn't need him anymore; he wanted someone younger than Loyle on the afternoon desk. Cursing at Patel, he stomped around in the mud room for a while, then busied himself by putting up the storms, clearing the vegetable bed, bleeding the furnace, cleaning his hunting rifles. After dinner and a few Manhattans, he was feeling better. They were having a good time watching that new quiz show, and he was finishing up on his Luger, when she went to the kitchen to mix another round. Someone on the TV shrieked, and she called to Loyle, "What's going on?" Then came a sound so loud it slammed her against the corner cabinet.

Through the pain, she called for Loyle. No one answered. Light and dark throbbed. Voices mumbled and receded. Jack came and went, then stayed. She'd had a stroke, they said. She'd hit her head.

"Where's Dad?"

"He's dead, Mom. He's gone."

"Your dad won't leave me." She tried not to wake up again.

After the hospital, after the convalescent center, Jack said she couldn't go home. He rented the house to her neighbor's no-account daughter and her two kids. "Just till you're stronger, Mom. Better to have the place occupied." She pictured balled-up socks in her bathroom and open cereal boxes littering her kitchen counter, but where she'd left Loyle watching TV, in the living room, she couldn't see. That was a void.

Jack said that's where she'd been found, not the kitchen, but she remembered the edge of the cupboard rushing at her and the bourbon cascading over the counter's edge. She'd only been gone a minute. She would be right back. Maybe Loyle tripped coming to help her, on that cheap, loose carpet, and stumbled into the TV tray. But uncertainty snagged beneath her heart and spread like black ink. They'd replaced the carpet two years ago. Before it was too late, she had to go home.

The next day, she phoned the house and got Luanne's daughter before she left for work. Betty said she wanted to come collect a few things, and not to worry about what the house looked like. "No, don't trouble yourself. I have a key."

The cab nosed over the dip at the end of the driveway, and Betty kept her eyes on Luanne's house, next door. Kitty litter bins were stacked on her kitchen steps. Since the accident, she'd been here once, with Jack, getting what he thought she'd want for The Courtyard, but she'd waited in the car, with the heater on. The taxi driver came around to open the door, and she forced herself to look out the windshield. The house looked the same, but not quite real, as if the windows didn't really open and there was nothing behind the white siding. She rocked herself out of the cab. A few flakes of late snow, small as soot, bit her face as she paid the cabdriver.

"Come for me in an hour and a half."

At the top of the stairs, in her backdoor window, a cardboard bunny, like ones in The Courtyard's dining room, was taped to the glass. She gripped the railing, shaken to find the steps that Loyle had put the safety treads on were now treacherous, but her key glided into the lock. Inside, in the gloom, she caught her breath, appalled by the changes: kids' dishes drying in the rack, a new TV where her breadbox used to be, on the refrigerator pictures of strangers. On one of her kitchen chairs, a red baby seat was strapped. When Jack was little, he had a maple high chair with ABC blocks painted on the back, above the spindles. Now he was old, bald, and fat as Poppa. She took off her gloves to touch the Formica table and a ghost of her hand wiping the table stirred. Fighting a wave of unsteadiness, she fixed her eyes on the sticky rings made by the transparent honey bear in the center of the table and unbuttoned her coat. Loosening her neck scarf, she glanced up at the cupboard she'd hit on her way down. It wasn't splintered or patched, or damaged in any way. The old cream paint, the same brass handle. "No, Mom, you hit your head on the coffee table." Her head rang. What else had she gotten wrong?

Three short steps to the archway that led to the living room. She closed her eyes and inched around the kitchen table. She could smell fresh paint, but this wasn't possible. Jack said he'd taken care of everything: paint, new carpet, a pair of couches that would do for Barbara and her kids. "It's all fresh, Mother. Everything had to go."

With her hand on the rough plaster, she felt a pressure like an avalanche and a roar that wasn't sound tremble through her. When it subsided, she opened her eyes. Unfamiliar shapes crouched in the dim light. Slowly, they gathered their edges together and became solid: Loyle's lounger, the TV tray in front, and her rose-colored chair. A highball glass gleamed where she'd set it on the flat wooden arm. Blue light sprang from the TV. Loyle leaned forward—he was in his lounger after all—his face was flushed.

"Oh, Lord, where have you been?" she said.

He struggled to get up and everything shook.

What's the point, that's what I want to know, what's the point? You understand me, Betty? You listening? He picked up his drink, ice cubes jangling, then smashed it down, and punched the air. Hell, when you're old, you've got no reason to be. It's as simple as that. The Eskimos were right. Put you on an ice floe, push off. There's nothing left. Nothing. Just a big nothing. She walked toward him, but he didn't see as he waved the Luger toward the credenza. Put that gun down, Loyle, you're upsetting me. Come on, Betty, take this, here, it's not too heavy for you, come here, I can't stand up, come here. I want you to end this right now Loyle. Stop Loyle. No, I'm serious, here. I won't. Look, let's go to bed. I don't want to leave without you. You're not going anywhere. Give me that gun Loyle. You're not going to. Give me . . . no . . . Loyle . . . I love you, Betty. She was reaching for the Luger, propping herself up on the arm of her chair, her damp hand grabbing the barrel, then slipping. Behind Loyle, the orange curtains flared and the room broke into flying shards.

She woke. She was sitting in an unfamiliar chair in her own living room. A playpen filled the corner near a monstrously big TV she'd never seen before. A shadow moved, Loyle in front of the TV. He beckoned to her.

"Thank God." She struggled to stand. Her head throbbed as she got to her feet and started toward him, but he vanished, like smoke.

"Come back," she whispered.

Don't want to leave without you.

His words hung before her, suspended, like a banner. Above her head, the ceiling vanished and she could see the sky, gold-streaked and soaring, with a speck, a chariot, arcing toward a burning radiance. She raised her arms and lifted off, her feet grazing the TV, and upward she flew, knocked every which way by turbulence, until she drew close to the racing sleigh, and her arms extended like ribbons to seize the reins streaming behind the winged white horse. She grabbed on tight. He would take her to Loyle.

A jolt traveled up her legs, jarring and real. She lost the reins and grasped at the rushing air, windmilling until she touched the back of a velvet chair. Stumbling backwards, she found herself jostled by cushions, chair cushions. Her old living room closed in around her and the shadowed ceiling dropped into place. The floor rumbled, the furnace kicking in. A moment later, warm air rushed over her ankles.

She wasn't supposed to be in this world. Loyle wanted her to follow him.

In the back room, the gun cabinet was empty. Of course, renting the house out, Jack would have put them in the basement.

She took the basement steps slowly, bringing both feet together, before lowering her right foot to the next. If she broke a hip, she'd never get another chance. At the bottom, she caught her breath. In front of the dryer, a laundry basket was heaped with green and brown children's clothes. Gone was the rack where she'd hung Loyle's soft plaid shirts warm from the dryer, their sleeves always folding forward dejected. Along the far wall, Jack had stacked boxes and labeled them in black marker. Dbl bed sheets, Sweaters, Dresser misc. He must have emptied the bedrooms to make way for Barbara and her kids. Mom's Shoes, Wearable. Mom's Shoes, Unwearable. Unwearable? She held onto the old bureau to fight the dizziness, then shook herself.

"Hurry, you're on a mission," she said out loud, for courage.

She found Loyle's things sandwiched behind the ironing board and the old drying rack. Dad's. Dad's. Dad's. Two boxes were marked Dad's weapons, a tall vertical one, probably the shotguns and rifles, and a short one, which she shimmied forward. Pain shot through her chest as she ripped open its top. Cleaning rags were stuffed around two rusted cans of oil, some odd-shaped parts she couldn't identify, and the butt of a fancy pearl-handled revolver he'd bought in Vegas. She wanted the Luger. Maybe the tall box. Widening her stance, she tugged it forward and pushed it over. The folded-in flaps spilled open and out fell his shotgun and hunting rifle cases. She kicked the guns aside and twisted the box, managing to upend it. A canister of movie film and a ballpoint pen clattered on the cement floor. No Luger.

Disappointed and breathless, she sank onto an old wooden chair. Where was it? Jack wouldn't have taken it with him and he wouldn't have stored it upstairs, not with kids. Looking at the shelves filled with jars of graying tomatoes and plums that no one would ever eat, she realized the gun was gone. The police had it. That's where it was. Why did she always understand things too late?

At the top of the stairs, she stared at the TV where her breadbox used to be. On crime shows, she'd seen duffel bags of guns traded in the backs of pawnshops. The noisy minute hand of the copper kettle-shaped clock jumped forward. She could get another Luger.

The phone book was still where it should be, in the bureau in the hall. She flipped to pawnshops and wrote down an address, which was right around the corner from the bank. In the back of her whatnot drawer, she found a half-filled pack of Loyle's bullets.

Above the sink a rusted wire, what was left of the bird feeder's hanger, tapped the window.

When the cab returned, she said, "Take me downtown first. I need to make a stop."

❖

She walked in the front of First Merchants' and out the side door. Liberty Pawn was dusty and narrow. The long side wall was hung with guitars in exotic colors and shapes, the back wall held lamps, TVs that couldn't work, old cash registers, safes, a silver cocktail set. She couldn't see any guns. From the back, she heard a TV.

She leaned on the long case and peered through the smudged glass at lockets, bracelets, wedding and engagement rings spread out on folds of gray velvet not so different from how they must have been displayed when each was new and caught the eye of a lover, who would have asked a salesman with smooth hands and deferential manner to lift it out, turn it this way and that in the light. Each dull and bent thing here had once sparkled, and sparkling, had been chosen to speak of desire and maybe commitment. Now each was a testament to failure. She fingered her own platinum band worn nearly to a sliver.

"Can I help you?" A pudgy Indian man smiled at her.

She stared at him, not knowing why she'd come. Behind him, the beaded curtain clicked and swayed. She heard Loyle chuckle and remembered.

"I'd like to buy a Luger."

"What is your purpose for wanting such?" Between his tiny teeth, a tongue darted to clear a crumb at the corner of his mouth.

She had to be careful. "For my husband," she said, touching her pearls to emphasize that she was old and harmless. "He had one from the War, but now we can't find it. It meant a lot to him."

He knit his brow, dubious.

"Actually, he doesn't know it's missing. I want to replace it before he notices. It was a souvenir, from his service in North Africa, just a souvenir."

He shrugged, bored, and retreated, moments later returning with a metal box. "Here." He unlatched the stiff catch and pulled out a dark, familiar pistol, bouncing it on his palm before handing it to her.

She reached for the Luger, hoping he would put her trembling down to old age. The gun was heavy and cold, its crosshatched grip like her old hatchet's, but it did look like Loyle's. She squinted at its surface, turning it over, worried that some differing detail would alert Loyle to the substitution, then remembered he wouldn't see it.

"Does it work?" she asked.

"You said it's for sentimental—"

"I just mean, is it in working order? Because if it isn't, my husband will know it's not his." Even to her ear it sounded like a lie.

He sighed. "Lady, I can't tell you what your husband will think. I tell you only that the mechanism works." He showed her a small button near the trigger, which he pressed with his thumb, then lifted the barrel and aimed toward the plate glass window. Click. Her heart jumped.

She said she'd take it.

It was much heavier than she'd imagined. She hid it in her weekend bag at the back of her closet. After that, whenever she left her room, she feared that some aide might snoop, or that the gun would go off spontaneously, or that it wasn't there at all, or that she'd imagined the pawnbroker, imagined the clicking curtain, imagined the gun's weight in her shopping bag. Then she would hurry back to check that the strand of orange yarn she'd draped over her suitcase was still in place. All the time she was excited and terrified. The hidden gun was like an extra heart pumping life into her worn-out body. She remembered a story from high school, about a beating heart trapped in the wall. At night, she woke to hear the gun, not beating, but emitting a low bass throb.

One afternoon, she locked her door and took the gun into her bathroom. Guns had to be oiled, that she knew from watching Loyle, but the Luger's design was tricky. She'd never be able to put it back together if she took it apart. Getting out her manicure kit, she applied Vitamin E cuticle oil to the surfaces she could reach with a Q-Tip, and wiped it dry, shaken by how like an animal it was, slipping in her hand, ferocious and malevolent. Hurriedly, she wrapped it in a hand towel and put it back, eager to get away from the gun, to the lounge, to talk to anyone.

In the corridor, she heard music, a tune of Glenn Miller's, coming from the community room. She paused, her heart quieting, and stepped closer. Inside the room, half a dozen women sat in chairs watching three couples dance in the open space: Sylvie with Harold Rasmussen, the Baileys, and Tony Vito with the newcomer with the wide hips and plump calves. Sylvie and Harold moved with the grace of refrigerators on coasters, but Tony, in his white shirt and red necktie, twirled the new woman with the style of a pro. The song ended. Tony bowed to his partner as one of the women on the sidelines approached for the next number, and straightening, noticed Betty. He grinned and waved for her to join them, but she backed away, her face flushing.

Jack called a week before Memorial Day and said he thought she should come for a visit.

She didn't want to see him. "I want to be here." Loyle was in the columbarium on the hill. "Everyone's going to the cemetery. The Center is putting on extra shuttles."

"Then I'll come up there."

She told him she'd just as soon be with her women friends; they were all widows, too. "Mom, this doesn't feel right."

"This is what I want. Now my TV show is about to come on, so I'm saying goodbye."

From the telephone rose the same plastic smell as the Plexiglas crib the first time the nurse had wheeled her son into her room. "Jack–"

"Yes, Mom?"

She knotted her hand into a fist. "I love you. Don't you ever, ever forget that."

The morning of the 28th was humid and hot, with the sun indistinct behind a gauzy haze. The shuttle was half full when Betty climbed on, clutching her purse heavy with the Luger and a small flag that came with a plastic holder to attach it to a wall. She was pleased to see the one single seat by the wheel hump was empty. After she sat down, Tony Vito walked on and took the seat behind her.

"Making the pilgrimage?"

She said nothing, but willed a barrier to rise from the back of her seat, like the divider in a limousine. He leaned forward, smelling of spearmint gum and the stench of an abandoned well.

"Don't mean to offend," he rasped, "last thing I'd want to do."

Betty shifted her purse. The brown-haired one from *Charlie's Angels* would swing around and have the gun drawn on him in a flash. "Back off, mister," she'd say. Betty faced forward, and nodded to the Ursos as they lumbered by. "Hello, hello." After they passed, Tony tapped her shoulder.

"Why don't you join us next time for a little 1-2-3?"

Betty lifted her chin with disdain and stared out the window at the bus' big convex mirror that warped the ground into a plane she could slide right off. The seat behind her squeaked as Tony withdrew.

No one spoke as the bus wound through town and into the country again. When they disembarked inside the gates of the cemetery, everyone scattered, Tony heading toward a far section near the pond. He still had a vigorous gait, from all that dancing.

In the shadowy columbarium, she was alone. After sticking the flag on the wall next to Loyle's plaque, she sat and watched light from above glide across the marble surfaces. Her parents were up on the hill, in the original section, in her mother's family plot. She opened her purse and gasped at the sight of the Luger. Why had she brought it? It was empty. What had she been thinking? She hid the gleaming metal barrel under a wad of Kleenex before ripping a blank check from her bankbook. "Cremate me and place my ashes next to Loyle's," she wrote, and stuck the note in her brassiere.

The sun's warmth felt good on her head, and she dozed, awakening with a start when the light was no more than a sliver in the far corner. Disconcerted by the silence, wondering if she'd only imagined Loyle beckoning to her, she walked to the cemetery's entrance, wishing for another sign. Except for a couple of people on the far side of the pond, the cemetery was empty. A sedan turned into the driveway and inched up the fork to the left, followed by two family vans, then disappeared over a hill. Quiet descended. Another shuttle would come, she told herself, sitting down on the bench, trying to quell a ripple of anxiety by reading the names on the monuments across the way: Holt, Mother and Father, Gerald Krause, Schuenmann. Before Loyle, she and her friends had come out here and gotten drunk and made up stories about the dead, trying to scare each other. She remembered Caroline's husky voice floating through the dark telling about Gerald Krause, decapitated in a plunge down the grain elevator, his blood staining an entire shipment of wheat. No problem. They sold it as red wheat after that.

At a sound, she jumped, her heart knocking wildly. "Who's there?"

"Tony Vito." He appeared by the stand of lilacs behind the bench enclosure. "Didn't scare you, did I?"

She scowled, pressing her bulging purse against her belly. If she had a heart attack, this would all be over, she thought, as he asked if he could join her. She gave a curt nod, wiping her lip.

"See your flag is gone."

Overhead leaves rustled.

"The 319th group, right?"

That was Loyle's outfit during the War. How did Tony know that? She looked directly at him. Once he must have been good looking, before his brow was tugged down by gravity, and his skin coarsened. Although his eyes were the indefinite stone-color all but the bluest eyes go, they were clear and intent, with an expression that made her look away.

"North Africa, right?" he said.

"Did you know Loyle?"

"Not well. Knew him some from the VFW."

"You weren't in the War."

He lifted his gaze to scan the road. "No, but for a while in the fifties, I supplied liquor to most of the clubs in central Wisconsin. So, I was . . . I guess, an honorary member, for a while." He pulled a handkerchief from his pocket and wiped his neck.

"So you knew him."

He worked his mouth, avoiding her eyes as he stuffed the handkerchief back. "I don't know why I said what I said about him. I know why, but . . ."

"Don't say anything. "

"But I was thinking maybe you and I could . . . Would you like to go on that trip to the Dixie Queen with me, next Saturday?"

She turned away and lifted her hand to her forehead, pretending to search for the shuttle.

"What do we have to lose, Betty? We haven't got all the time in the world."

"I'm not interested." She clutched her purse, feeling the gun against her ribs, and began walking to the gate. It wasn't fair that she'd had been left behind to face this.

"A few laughs, that's what I'm saying. It's not too late for a few laughs."

She reached the gate, and clung to the iron bars, praying the shuttle would appear by the time she counted to ten. One. Two. Three. A grackle tore at something by the road. Behind her she heard Tony mutter something, then a branch snap. Five. Six. Seven.

After dinner, she hung the Do Not Disturb sign on her door. She laid her good dress on the bed and her patent leather pumps on the floor. From her bedside table drawer, she retrieved the letter she'd written, adding a postscript about interring her remains by Loyle's. This she propped next to her jewelry box. Beneath her malachite necklace she found her favorite picture of her and Loyle—they were sitting in a pontoon boat in the Dells—and a trace of memory swept over her, of how it felt to be full of life and sure it would never end. She wiped her eyes and lifted the picture close to examine Loyle's expression. Her heart began to knock against the steel-cold bars in her chest.

From her purse, she took out the Luger, and from the inside pouch of her weekend bag, the bullets. She set everything on a paper towel on her bedside table. Although her fingers had begun to shake, she found the two indentations in the sides of the grip that released the magazine and inserted the bullets the way she'd practiced, relieved by each tiny, satisfying click.

Now her whole body was shaking. Carefully, she made her way to the cupboard where she'd hidden the plastic flask of Elijah Craig behind her family albums. Concentrating hard because her fingers refused to work, she opened the mini-fridge and mixed herself a Manhattan, then wrestled with the ice tray to pop out a few cubes. Plink. Plink. They jostled merrily. She took a sip and felt the warmth slide into her belly and loosen her limbs. She turned off the lights and sat at the table. Even in the dark, the Luger shone.

Some one tapped on her door. "It's me, Tony. About earlier. . ."

"Go away." She took another sip. The alcohol made the back of her tongue heavy the way sex once had. The shadow under her door pulled away.

The scent of the bourbon swirled around her, fermented of night and lipstick and sweaty jazz. She could smell Loyle's thick black hair and his young body. They were swaying together in the dark, lights spangled on the river behind him, they would never change, or have a baby who would become a stranger, and they wouldn't grow old, and he would never leave her, and he would never break promises or ask too much of her, but they would remain like this, clothes slipping under their hands. And she would never have to practice the two-finger movement, thumb and index finger, required to release, then pull a trigger, or turn a gun inward on herself and bite the barrel, pressing it up slightly, until she could feel it rest against the roof of her mouth, or wait for her deaf neighbor to turn up the volume on his TV so the rumble of canned laughter was louder than the hum of the air conditioner, and a shot would sound like another TV noise. She would never have to do any of this.

The Sweet Collapse of the Feeble

THROUGH THE CURTAIN ABOVE THE sink, I see Civility tug off the bandana that's keeping her black curls in check and amble toward the stool under the sycamore. Since she took up boxing, she walks like a sailor with a wide, rolling gait. The afternoon sun is full on the ring set up at the back of the yard, and that new sparring partner Fletcher hired, who's a head taller than Civility but kind of bent looking, is pacing around the canvas, jabbing in the air, trying to knock out flies, looks like.

Two months it's been since Civility got home from the army, all excited about becoming a prizefighter. Two weeks after that Fletcher Weekley drove up with a U-Haul full of equipment, and Civility introduced him as her trainer. Since then it's been one thing after another. Fletcher's got Civility training six, seven hours a day, sprints, foot work, weights, working out on the speed bag, sparring. Her first match is coming up in Nashville in less than two weeks.

The army is supposed to settle the young. I had my hopes. Before Civility went in, she was as wild as a good girl can get and still be called good. Now she's back, I do see a change. She's surer; she's got focus. I wish it weren't boxing, but still.

"Bernice, doesn't your granddaughter look like something?" I say out loud. "A hundred and fifty-five pounds of pure muscle. She carries it well, wouldn't you say? Not mannish, not really. Just ... well ... extra shapely, although those quads are right at the edge of getting out of hand."

Bernice, my momma, doesn't say anything. High on top of the twenty-five-cubic-foot, stainless steel, frost-free, side-by-side refrigerator with the ice, water, and juice dispensers right in the door, Bernice keeps her own counsel in her gold plastic urn. Civility bought me the refrigerator with her discharge pay, as a coming home present. She says she doesn't like it serving as a shrine to Bernice. But then, she and Bernice never did get along.

I miss Bernice. But one good thing about her being dead: I can speak my mind, something I got precious little opportunity to do when she was alive. Bernice would certainly have had something to say about this prize-fighting business. I don't know exactly what. She could have gone any number of ways, but she would have said something.

Out the window I hear Fletcher hoot. I flick the curtain aside and see he's got his arm around Civility's shoulder. He's a tall, low-hipped Texan with a wind-scorched face and hair going to gray. A little oily. He smells the way boys who were aiming for prison did when I was growing up. Fletcher Weekley is the kind of bad choice Civility always used to make.

"Bernice, there are times when I wish you were still here. I'd like to see you put Fletcher Weekley straight." I let the curtain drop and turn to look in Bernice's direction. Up on top of the refrigerator that gleams like it's still in the showroom, her urn catches a slant of light and winks at me.

The first night after Civility came home, she went for some ice. "My god, this is prehistoric. Here's my Peaches 'n Champagne lipstick from behind this spinach bag covered in ice. You haven't defrosted this monster since I left home." Looking into the tiny mirror by the sink, she put some on.

I didn't say anything. Of course I defrosted the freezer. I just always put the lipstick back.

After they hooked up this new icebox, Civility and I put strawberry daiquiris in the juice dispenser.

"I wonder what Bernice would say if she could see us now, you all grown up, and buying me this fancy icebox, us having a drink together, you legal."

"Oh, she'd find something to complain about. I sure hated how she ran roughshod over you."

"She did not."

"She did, too. And here she is, long dead, and you're still listening to her, aren't you?"

"I talk to her. For companionship, like TV. She doesn't talk back. I have asked her what she thinks of your boxing. She hasn't said a word."

"I don't believe it, Bernice silent as the tomb?" Civility laughed, giving me a stab of shame, since Bernice was long overdue in her tomb. But before I could dwell on that, Civility crossed her arms and fixed her eyes on me. "Fact is, I don't care for her or anyone else's opinion about my boxing."

I hadn't said a word.

A week later Fletcher Weekley showed up.

Through the screen I watch Fletcher push on Civility's gloves. He spotted her boxing in a gym near her base in Texas, told her she should take up fighting seriously, should take him on to manage her. Sold his Go-Kart track—it was probably failing anyway—to come and train her. Civility calls this commitment.

"That is one no-account man," I say to Bernice, though she's heard it before. I can practically hear her snort every time he walks into this kitchen. I wouldn't say this out loud, but Fletcher reminds me of Bernice's last husband, Harlan Soames, a country club car dealer from Murfreesboro. A different cut of society he was, but with the same glad-handing ways.

Out back I see my girl and the new sparring partner circling each other. They're both keeping low, moving like scorpions. With the headgear hiding their faces, all you can see is the concentration. Civility has always been a big girl, taking after Bernice, but now she has a honed look, hard and sure. I'm proud of her, I really am, I just wish it wasn't boxing that had brought on her resolve.

That other girl lands one in Civility's ribs. I look away, up at Bernice, and when I turn back to the window, I see Civility is too open, trying to get back, but that girl comes in quick with an uppercut missing its power. Civility dances away, collecting herself. Both of them are sweating good now, and Fletcher yells something I don't catch. I can't stand to watch Civility get hit. Fletcher says I should get used to it, but Civility says not to bother because it's not going to happen often.

She's tight now, working hard, arms lumpy with muscle, lots of quick jabs. That other girl is even tireder than she. Civility walks her around the ring, then lands one on her headgear. Fletcher steps into the ring and the girls stop and jiggle their arms. Fletcher takes them to the corner, gives them a drink of water.

Through the window, I call to them. "Dinner in about an hour?"

Fletcher hands each of the girls a towel, making a joke, I can tell, before he answers me. "That'll be just fine, ma'am," he says in that smarmy tone.

When I told Civility that Fletcher was too old and used-up for her she just laughed and laughed, saying he was only her manager and trainer. I doubt Fletcher knows that.

I ease open the fridge door, to get out the fish. With the old one, the door practically glided open and Bernice rested easy on top, like a baby in a Cadillac. With this new icebox, you have to be careful. I am constantly worried I'll forget, or someone else will, and pull too hard, and Bernice will land on the floor. I keep her here rather than on the coffee table in the living room, because she's closer. Besides, she had a real taste for ice cream.

After dinner, while we're washing up and Fletcher is lounging in front of the TV, Civility says, "About this trip to Nashville."

I shut off the water, hoping she's having second thoughts about launching her boxing career, but I keep my face real neutral. You push Civility in one direction, and she'll aim in the other.

"Come with us. I know you said you wouldn't, but come." My heart lurches. My baby girl wants me to come. Then she adds, "Nashville's not that far from Murfreesboro."

"About an hour and a half, I believe," I say, wiping down the sink. Murfreesboro is where Bernice lived the short while she was married to Harlan Soames and that's where her will says she's to be buried.

"Momma, you can't keep her up on the refrigerator forever."

"Having Bernice's ashes up there is a comfort to me. What do you care? You'll be moving on."

Civility crosses her arms, making a show of her patience. "Momma, you know you have to do it. The Soames are holding a spot for her. We'll be in Nashville, which is less than an hour from Murfreesboro."

"When'd you become a travel agent?"

"We can stay on an extra day after my fight."

Fletcher appears in the doorway. His shiftless eyes slide back and forth between Civility and me. "Something wrong?"

"Nothing's wrong," I say.

He looks at Civility, and she looks to the top of the fridge. "I'm trying to convince Momma to lay Bernice's ashes to rest."

"Seems to me the women in your line don't know when to cut the apron strings. That's what I say." He flips the toothpick from one side of his mouth to the other.

I slap down the tea towel. "I don't believe I asked for your views, Fletcher Weekley."

Civility gives my shoulders a little squeeze. "Give it some thought, will you?"

"We better head out," Fletcher says, holding up their jackets. My daughter slips into the purple satin one, chain-stitched on the back with 'Sweet Civility'.

The screen door bounces shut behind them.

When Bernice was alive, most afternoons she and I'd sit at the kitchen table, surrounded by a cloud of smoke from her unfiltered Luckys, and we'd play double solitaire. Or sometimes she'd spread out fortune telling cards. This kind of mumbo-jumbo came naturally to Bernice. Or she'd read my hand. I remember how warm her touch was. She'd bend my fingers back, ever so gently, and say, "You're too stiff here. These fingers don't have any give, means you're never going to change. You'll always be what you are today. You didn't get my genes there, I can tell you that. Now, your right hand, that's better. Maybe there's hope. But in my experience, you can water the Sahara, but it'll still be a desert." Then she'd fold my hands in hers, taking away the sting.

It's pitch black outside when I hear the back door creak open and close. Civility tiptoes to my bedroom. "Momma?" She knows I'm awake. She sits beside me, blocking my view of my alarm clock.

"It's long past time to settle Grandma's ashes."

We both listen to the clock numbers flip over.

"Never mind what Fletcher said." She touches my cheek. "It is time. Come with us to Nashville."

I say I will.

As the day approaches, I'm on edge about everything: Civility in the ring with some stranger who won't stop; Civility and Fletcher in the hotel, even with separate rooms, even with me keeping an eye; and me delivering Bernice to the Soames, but I nestle my momma in my suitcase, and we set out. Fletcher's in the backseat with headphones on, and Civility drives, talking a mile a minute while I watch those white stripes on the road get sucked under the car.

The next day after breakfast, while Civility is tied up with the masseuse and Fletcher's on the phone, I steam the wrinkles out of her purple satin Everlast trunks and decide I'll take Bernice out to Murfreesboro, now, without them. I don't want Fletcher making smart-alecky remarks. I don't want Civility telling me what to do. I pop my head in Civility's bedroom and say I'm going to Murfreesboro. My daughter barely waves.

Once on the highway, with Bernice strapped in the passenger seat beside me, my nerves thin out and start to hum, like wind in the phone lines. I feel bad about my momma and bad about Civility. I wish I weren't dropping off Bernice with no ceremony, and so far from home. I wish Civility hadn't gotten this bug about prizefighting. And I wish I weren't going to be so alone. Resisting tears keeps me steady on the interstate and the two-lane stretch that leads to the gates of the Blessed Faithful Cemetery.

The man in the office asks if I'd like to drive out to the Soames mausoleum before filling out the papers. I say yes and he traces the way on a big map under glass on the counter. Lawn mowers cut the quiet as I drive extra slow along the row of mausoleums: Knopp, Pierce, Hutcheson, Winnard, Soames, the letters of that hateful name dripping stain. There it is.

Fly to Egypt, I think.

"I'd no more do that than fly to Egypt," Bernice would say when something was impossible. She used this expression long after men had flown to the moon, annoying the hell out of me, but that's what I think as I stare at the windowless granite box, with a metal grate for a door. I can no more lay my mother there, for all of eternity, than I can fly to Egypt.

I call out to the man standing in the office door, "I've changed my mind."

When I get back to the hotel, I don't bother to mention I've still got Bernice. That evening, when the three of us enter the arena from the parking lot full of fancy painted vans, I see the poster for tonight's events. Five wrestling matches open the evening, then comes Sweet Civility vs. LingLing, the Oriental Flower, the first of three boxing bouts. What stops me cold is a picture of the wrestlers, what Bernice would call "bare-assed women."

"Come on, Momma," Civility says, noticing where I'm looking. "That's just to bring in the crowd." Fletcher leads us into a dark hallway. "Once women's boxing takes off, they won't book it with the wrestling."

What bothers me is that she doesn't mind being on the same bill with Hells-a-poppin' Helen and Sweet Georgia Brown who's got two tiny breasts painted into the 'w' of Brown.

Next to a wall covered with electrical switches, a group of white trash men with stringy hair are sipping beer from bottles. Some of them are wearing leather vests over their bare chests. I swear a couple of them must have whole boxes of Kleenex stuffed into the fronts of their pants. Maybe yams.

Fletcher ushers us into a dressing room. Civility's in high color, prancing around, opening the closet doors, staring at herself close-up in the mirror, and Fletcher's already on the phone. In walk a couple of women in tight shorts, friends of his, and a couple of fat men in black T-shirts. Soon as Fletcher hangs up, he comes over to where I stand by the door. "Civility needs to be alone now." There are six people in here now, not counting him, Civility, and me, but I agree. He says to one of the fat men, "This is Civility's mother. You take her to my seats and bring her whatever she wants to drink. On me."

I follow this fellow out the door, and Civility rushes over. "Wish me luck, Momma."

"I love you, sugar pie, and wish you all the luck in the world," though I doubt that she and I mean the same things by "luck."

The wrestling is as bad as anything you see on TV. The announcer makes jokes, and in one match, one of the wrestlers is really a man dressed up as a woman.

After the wrestling is over, Civility and the girl she's fighting, LingLing the Oriental Flower, walk down the aisle. I feel as if I've swallowed a cantaloupe whole. Civility, bouncing up and down on those dainty white shoes, is in her purple and white, LingLing's in black and red. All Civility's assurances that she won't get hurt, that she's tough, that she's unstoppable, vanish and I'm scared. LingLing flips her waist-long hair around before knotting it up. The spotlights swim around the ring. Civility's dark curls shine. She's radiant. She's grinning as if she's already won. I try to make out LingLing, but she's coolly staring down the crowd.

Fletcher calls Civility back to her corner, takes off her robe. Her hands are taped and he slips on her gloves, checks them, and sets her headgear on tight. The referee calls the two girls into the center before releasing them. The bell rings.

Before either one of them lands a punch, I feel nervy, but I admit both girls are fine-looking. It's almost a pleasure to watch them mince around, eyeing each other, trying little moves. At first Civility is hanging back. She gets off a couple of quick jabs, then connects with an uppercut that sends LingLing reeling. I'm surprised to find myself screaming. LingLing hunches tight and comes back at Civility. They start swinging, those mean chops right from the shoulder, and when they land, beads of sweat fly and hang bright as diamonds in the light. After a lot of back and forth, they fall together, punching the other's back, and the referee breaks them apart. They move more slowly now, taking measure, and LingLing hits Civility square in the throat. I want to throw up. The bell rings.

Sitting on their stools without their headgear—Civility is in the opposite corner from where I sit—both girls are pale. The crowd screams advice. Civility sips water and bends her head to Fletcher. A little boy wipes her neck with a wet rag. She looks very, very far away.

I'm not ready for the bell to ring, but Civility settles the strap under her chin and comes out quickly, looking determined. Right at this point, watching Civility's sure moves, I am wonder-struck. Her power and her grace, where did they come from? In these past months of watching her, I don't believe I've really seen her.

"That's my daughter," I yell in a rush of mother tiger love. I want LingLing to die.

They're stumbling, swinging wildly, big purposeless throws, dumb as cows.

When the third round ends, both girls turn back to their own corners, sagging. The crowd simmers down. It's over. The air above the ring is misty. Civility can barely keep her head up. She lets herself be wiped down. Fletcher pours water over her face and he's talking but she's not listening. I don't know who won and I don't care.

A bunch of men standing by the ring call over the referee. I'd forgotten about judges, about there being something official going on. The girls are suddenly alert, both tossing their hair and flexing their arms. A microphone is lowered and the referee grabs it, waving my girl and the other into the center of the ring. "The winner is . . . " He swivels around waiting for the crowd to quiet some. "The winner is Sweet Civility." He lifts her arm.

She starts dancing a little twisty step, pumping her arms above her head, waving and laughing. Fletcher comes out and kisses her, and she looks for LingLing. Strobes are flashing and Civility spins back to the crowd and starts skipping around the ring, smiling at everyone.

I'm churned up. I'm glad she won; I didn't want her to lose. But winning. . . . Maybe if she'd lost, she wouldn't keep going. So, I'm sorry at least as much as I'm happy.

I wait where I am, figuring she'll want time alone with Fletcher. The next match begins and ends without me seeing anything, just hearing the bells. Before the main event, I walk to the dressing rooms. The halls are crowded with more white trash and black men in sunglasses. Civility's door is closed. I knock, and after a few seconds, it opens. She's dressed in her turquoise jumpsuit, her hair wet from the shower, her face flushed a livid purple with deep wrinkles pulling down around her nose and mouth. She looks as old as Bernice, but huge, bigger than I remember, and her dark eyes are teary and bloodshot. She hangs back a little. She's waiting to see if I'm upset. I'm afraid of getting this wrong, so I reach for her and hold her tight. She's taller than me by a couple of inches and as hard as a tree. I say that she was great, that she was much better than the other girl, that I'm proud of her, so proud I could bust. It's true, but it doesn't feel true.

When we move apart, I feel awkward, like a liar, and I ask where Fletcher is.

"He's gone off. Actually, I sent him off. Told him I'd see him in the morning."

So Fletcher's in the doghouse.

She says something about getting something to eat, but I'm thinking about Fletcher. "Did he take the car?"

She flips me the car keys. "He took my gear back to the hotel, in a taxi. Now let's get some Dairy Queen."

Happy to have my daughter to myself, I follow her past the men clogging up the corridor. The security guard holds open the door to the parking lot where the night air feels cool and clean. Civility slumps against the car and tilts her head back, her springiness drained away.

"You okay, sugar?"

"Let's just go. You drive."

This Dairy Queen sits in a yellow halo of parking lot lights, high on a ridge. Out back, past the dumpsters and a clump of oaks, the ground slopes away into brush. I look up at the cherry-colored sky, trying to pretend I'm not worried as Civility walks ahead, stiff-legged and hurting, towards an empty table.

I order two Blizzards and a butterscotch sundae. We eat in silence, me making my sundae last through her two shakes, and I think I can hear a small stream not too far away. By the time she finishes a third Blizzard, has a couple of Dilly Pies—Bernice favored Dilly Pies—and is debating what she wants next, she's got her color back.

"You're feeling better?" I ask.

She turns to me and puts her hand on my arm; her fingers are icy cold from holding all that ice cream. "Momma, I've got to tell you something." She looks past me, as if she'd afraid to look me in the eye, and I'm alarmed. "I don't want you to think I am who I was. I don't want you to think I can't stick to anything."

"What are you talking about, sugar? There's nothing you. . ." I'm talking too fast and she stops me, taking my hands in her knobby, rough paws.

"Momma, I've decided that this prizefighting is just going to be something to tell my children, some day. I had one fight and I'm glad I won, but that's it."

Time takes a couple of beats before I squeeze her hands. "Darling," I whisper, hugging her. Our hips knock and my arms don't reach all the way around her. My baby. I feel a great, swelling pride in her capability, in her sureness, but she frightens me, too. Who is this child of mine?

Looking over her shoulder, I see headlights from an incoming pickup sweep over our car and remember Bernice is still in the trunk. I close my eyes, dismissing her, and say, "Civility, you make your own decisions. You're grown now."

"Momma, you're not worried I'll jump around from one thing to another?"

"Am I sorry my only daughter has decided not to be boxer? Are you kidding?"

We laugh and head toward the bin to toss out our cups.

"I'm getting like you," she says.

"How's that?"

"Wondering what Bernice would say about this. 'Course she'd complain about my fighting, then tell me I'm a quitter. She had to decide everything for everybody." She stops the swinging top of the garbage bin. "Sorry, Momma, I forgot. How'd it go at the cemetery?"

"She's . . . I don't have any doubt Bernice would be glad, real glad, about you're not being a fighter, but she's. . . ."

Civility's guessed. She glares at me, and I feel how LingLing must have felt. "I drove to Murfreesboro and I couldn't do it."

"Why not?"

"She was never meant to rest with the Soames. I can't leave her in that stone-cold dead place."

Civility stares at me. "Momma, you are crazy. You have got to let go." When I don't say anything, she goes on, "I can tell you one thing, we are not driving her home with us. Give me those keys." She sticks out her hand.

I ignore her. I walk to the car—I'm stiff—and open the trunk where the gold dome's little belly button gleams in the center of the spare.

"Okay," I say, and pull the urn out, suddenly feeling very strong, as strong as Civility. No. That's not right at all. I'm not strong at all. What I feel is a rushing in my limbs, like the sweet collapse of the feeble. Civility leans against the car and lets me pass.

I am on my own. I stalk to where the yellow light falls off and keep walking past the dumpster, into the woods on the far side of the ridge. Thorny canes catch my skirt. I keep walking. When the ground turns soft, I hear a creek somewhere nearby, a reassuring sound that keeps going and going, like a momma clucking at her baby.

It's dark and I can't see much, but I unscrew the lid and there's a tiny rattle, teeth maybe, or bone.

"Right here, I'm laying you down, Momma," I say, but I don't feel anything important, just unbearably tired. I start to sing, "Precious Jesus, let me live my life in thee," and lift the urn up—it's not heavy, it's not light—and swing my arm in as wide an arc as I can manage, and there she goes, sifting into the air, drifting full wide between the trees and over the brush, and out across the creek I can't see, toward the distant houses with the lighted windows, through the night, maybe flying all the way to Egypt.

Civility comes up behind me and takes the urn and lid from my hands and puts them down on the ground. She holds my hand, and together we sing the first verse of "Precious Jesus." Neither one of us knows the words to what comes after.

The Collaborator

"DAVEEN, A WORD."

Down the narrow hall of faculty offices huffed Warren Hartz, art department chairman and chief of the silverback gorillas. Daveen unlocked her door and stationed herself half-in, half-out, blocking entry to her office. He put his hand on the doorjamb to catch his breath, then nodded toward her open office.

"I can't," she said, forcing friendliness into her voice. "My photo class begins in fifteen minutes."

"Yes, of course," he said, resettling his glasses, then fixed his eyes on a point somewhere behind her right ear. "About what happened." He paused. What had just happened was that her colleagues on Mel Vincent's tenure committee had reacted as if she were a feminist dinosaur, small brain, big tail, when she'd insisted they request a copy of the Dean's file on Mel. "As I said in the conference room, I will make the request, but I assure you, rumors is all it's ever been. Nothing more."

"So much more reason to turn over every stone—" She pictured mealy bugs scattering from a damp spot. "Since there have been rumors."

His chin jutted forward in annoyance. "I think you need to be careful about taking too . . . well, the only word is 'strident' a position. You've got to remember that you're going to have lunch with these colleagues for many years."

She had to admire the way he buried a threat inside concern, but it was that exact image, lunch into perpetuity, that made her want to leap from her office window.

" 'Due diligence,' what the handbook requires, is all I'm seeking, Warren. This is being professional, not strident." She made an effort to smooth her face, then lifted the corners of her mouth, approximating a smile.

"Professional," he echoed, looking directly at her. "All right. Good, now that I have your assurance, Daveen." He nodded and marched away.

Inside her office, she flung Mel's tenure application packet onto her desk, certain she'd made a wrong turn somewhere, though she wasn't sure where. Was it going into teaching in the first place? Was it landing in this lousy department? Or was it middle age? She glanced at her Linhof, her old field camera, which she'd consigned to bookend status long ago. In the dull afternoon light, the tidy, square box covered in mint-green leather with its lens concealed behind a fold-up front panel looked more like a 1960s woman's purse than a serious camera. Once when she and Mel were friends, she'd taken his picture with it on the fire escape outside the faculty lounge. Though she had eight years on him and a hell of a lot better exhibition record, they'd become allies, the youngest members of the under-budgeted and deeply conservative Art Department. That was before she'd seen him with the Asian student at the Cineplex, before he was caught in the RA's room, before his affair with Mindy Ott in her seminar class. Her worn copy of *Visual and Other Pleasures* slid sideways when she picked up the Linhof, blew off the dust, unlatched the front panel, and carefully, because she was out of practice, hooked the lens board to the focusing rack, a mini train track. After graduate school, she'd bought the camera for a project at an archeological dig in Provence. She racked out the lens, crackling the stiff leather bellows, and remembered that hot summer, the golden dust of the excavation that created a haze in her pictures that, one critic wrote, "resonated with the mystery of history lost." She could remember the stifling heat under the black cloth, she could remember rising at four thirty in the morning, before the workers, to get the dawn light, but she could no longer remember what it was like to love her work.

When Daveen rolled in the slide projector cart, her Intermediate Photography students were lounging around the seminar table they'd already littered with soda cans and rumpled snack bags. The sleepiest rested their heads on their backpacks, but most straightened when she read the attendance list: "Tanya, Andrew, E.J., Will, Larissa, Kuwon, Christophe, no Christophe today, okay, Julie." The door creaked open. A hand appeared, followed by a ragged sleeve, then the epaulette of a military jacket, Christophe Artaud's, the consistently late French student. He stepped in, slid along the wall, and miming abject apology, pulled the knitted cap from his head so that his coarse black hair stood up in spikes. Looking more tubercular than ever, he wiped his rabbity nose with a chapped knuckle and slipped into the chair next to Julie.

"Sorry I am late again. The bus, it didn't come."

Almost, Daveen thought, a French accent almost redeems a feeble excuse. She tried to begin a discussion on portraiture, but Christophe had everyone's attention as he wrestled his notebook from his jacket pocket, pretending it was alive and angry. "When you're ready, Christophe, we're going to discuss photographic portraiture." She looked around. When she began teaching twelve years earlier, she'd been astonished that she could earn a living talking about photography. "What's a portrait?"

Predictably, wan Larissa said that it was a picture of a person.

"Could a part of a person, hands or something, be a portrait?" asked someone near the window.

She spoke about synecdoche, the detail that signified the whole, remembering the photograph she'd taken of Mel six years ago, a black and white close-up of the back of his head, his short hair shining like a Weimaraner's coat. "Of course, it's recognizable," she'd told him. "Anyone can tell it's you by these bumps behind your ears." Since he'd shaved his head, the bumps were more prominent than ever she'd noticed sitting two rows behind him at the last faculty meeting. They hadn't spoken in two years.

Laughter broke out, bringing her back to the classroom. "What I'd like us to attend to, however, is likeness." Larissa wrote "likeness" in her notebook, and Daveen went on, trying not to sound like a recording. "The most memorable portraits often show more than what a person looks like. They suggest something of spirit or character, and often, with celebrities, something of the myth."

"Like Annie Leibowitz's of Sting?" Julie asked, flicking her long silver nails in Christophe's direction. Daveen dimmed the room lights and turned on the slide projector.

Greta Garbo's sculpted face glowed in the dark: Steichen, for *Vanity Fair*. 1928. Click, up came the Avedons: Truman Capote, Gwyneth Paltrow, Laurie Anderson. About each Daveen mentioned some fact, when and how it was made, or the reasons it had become significant, hearing the scratch of pens as they wrote in their notebooks, aware of how reductive her words were, how misleading. What swept over her as she looked at each photograph was something she used to feel with her own work, how every picture made was, in truth, an act of love. With her old Linhof, her battered Olympus, two Rolleis, the Horseman, she had made love to the world. Now she no longer made good images, or, for that matter, any images. Where had it all gone? The tidal surge in her work had carried her this far, then left her stranded on a tiny island she wasn't suited for, someone at odds with her colleagues, a teacher of indifferent students, whose heads now glowed bluewhite and vacant in the reflected light of the screen. Not knowing if they were listening, she went on, "In the most memorable portraits, you, we, the viewers, sense a relationship between the sitter and the photographer, who stands in our place. This relationship springs up between the photographer who courts revelation and recognizes it, and the sitter's willingness to display or withhold in a visible way. This interaction between what the sitter reveals and what the photographer sees could be called a collaboration."

Or a gift, a gift that can be snatched away. Daveen flipped on the room lights and blinked under the sudden illumination.

"Can we take a break?" Julie asked, standing and flashing her navel ring before Daveen could ask for a response. The others stretched and began to rifle in their bags for cigarettes and change.

Disappointed to have lost the chance to find out if anything she'd said had gotten through, she said, "Ten minutes, no more. We have a lot to cover today." Turning, she almost knocked into Christophe, 6'5", maybe more. Rattled, she said, "What's up, Chris?"

"I wanted to ask you about what is it you mean by 'collaboration.'"

His accent made her think of Vichy France and Cartier-Bresson's photographs of collaborators fending off accusers after the Liberation. When she'd studied black-and-white movies of that era in graduate school, she'd like to imagine herself in the Resistance, if she'd been alive, if she'd been French. "The word means something slightly different in French. What I mean by collaboration is that when a photographer is able to draw another person, a sitter, into a moment of disclosure, the photograph will bear the imprint not only of the disclosure, but of the dance between photographer and sitter. This dance can be very subtle. It may not be physical, although it may, as in camera point of view and angle, closeness or distance, and it may be subtle, but it is always mental. A connection. Collaboration."

A smile spread slowly across his face, cutting folds in his cheeks, like those of an older man, and his tea-colored eyes held her as if they were sharing a joke.

Had she missed something? She asked if he understood what she meant.

"Oh, yes," he answered, with a supercilious quirk of his mouth.

Certain she'd missed something, and feeling dense, she watched him wipe his nose again and decided whatever it was wasn't worth pursuing. "Well, then . . . I'm going to get a cup of coffee."

In the hall, she passed Julie, and a moment later heard her talking to Christophe, then laughter. She stiffened, certain they were talking about her until she identified in Julie's high, rushed voice and Christophe's languorous response the duet of flirtation, unmistakable, even at a distance. Around the corner, E.J. and Larissa, heads close, slouched beside the water fountain, and beyond them, another couple whispered to each other, the boy's hands in the girl's jean pockets, pressing her to him. How could she hope to teach issues of representation and visual meaning while her students were bobbing on a sea of hormones and desire? Only forty and she'd already forgotten.

Pulling open the glass door to the Art Department's office suite, she saw Warren at the secretary's desk looking at a computer printout and thought, the pheromones stop here.

"Daveen, I'm glad to run into you. By a miracle, I mean a miracle, the Dean responded immediately to my call. Tomorrow they will send up the file you insisted upon."

If miracles were possible, she wouldn't be here.

The other members of Mel's tenure committee were already seated around the conference table when she arrived: Chuck Miller, sculpture, Juan Gutierrez, graphic design, and Sylvia Vass, the outsider from Journalism. Through dusty Venetian blinds, sunlight raked across the room. The film noir lighting and the sudden silence made her suspicious, so when her apologies for getting waylaid by a student didn't prompt the usual chorus of sympathetic complaints about students, she knew they had been talking about her. As Warren passed the Dean's file to Chuck on his left without a word, she remembered his unusual cheerfulness earlier. It seemed to Daveen that Chuck only pretended to read it, before handing it to Sylvia. Had Warren already shared it with him? No one spoke as the file made the rounds. When it got to Daveen, she felt the others' eyes on her as she flipped through copies of self-evaluations written over the past five years, three chairman's reviews, all good, and a letter written in a large, juvenile script on ruled paper, signed by a Heidi Cole. Nothing on Mindy Ott, or the Asian student—Michiko something—or the RA fiasco, or the others that Daveen had heard about. But Heidi Cole, whoever she was, had written that Mel had detained her in the studio one night.

I pushed him off and ran for the door. I didn't want to go back to class the next week, but I didn't want to flunk the class, so I kept going. But I always made my friend stay with me, even when we went on break. He gave me a C, only because I wouldn't sleep with him. I deserved at least a B.

The note was dated two and a half years ago. Attached was a memo in the Dean's hand asking Warren to look into the matter. Warren's note, dated a week later, stated that he'd "interviewed the parties and found no merit to the young woman's claims."

Chuck, across the table, and Juan, on her right, seemed to be waiting for her to respond. Irritated to give them the satisfaction, she set the file down with the girl's letter on top.

"Warren, could you tell us what this Heidi Cole said when you met with her?"

He smiled as if she'd moved her pawn in the wrong direction. "Very vague girl. She admitted that Mel didn't touch her. She felt 'trapped', " he raised his voice into a falsetto parody of the girl, "but couldn't say exactly what Mel did that made her feel that way. Something about his standing too close. I explained that Mel had a very personal approach to teaching, that he was known for getting close to his students."

Exactly.

"Then the girl got teary and said she didn't want him to lose his job. I had the definite impression that she'd started all this because she was disappointed with her grade. Of course, I also spoke to Mel." Warren smiled and looked directly at Daveen. "He assured me there was nothing to the girl's charges."

"Assured you?" Daveen glanced at Sylvia for corroborating indignation, but Sylvia pretended to be lost in thought. Daveen redirected her attention to Warren. A spasm of irritation twitched at his eye.

"He did indeed. I have the utmost faith in my faculty."

"People have been known to lie about sex," Daveen said.

"The girl told me quite clearly that Mel never asked for sex. And, as I was trying to say, he'd known she wanted a B, she'd begged for one, but he in good conscience couldn't give her one."

"Good conscience" should turn his mouth to stone, Daveen thought, as he folded his hands on the table, smiled serenely, and asked, "Do any of you know this young woman, Heidi Cole?"

Chuck answered so quickly she knew this had been arranged. "She was in my foundation drawing class, and she's a . . . " He worked his lips in contempt, telegraphing his effort at restraint, because of her presence and Sylvia's. "She's a flirt."

"A flirt? My god, Chuck—"

"That's what I said." He glared at her.

"I looked into it," Warren snapped.

Daveen locked her eyes on a couple of bent hairs at the top of Warren's head, which shook like antennae as he emphasized each word. "This was not a serious charge. And Daveen, I might ask myself, if I were you," he paused, "why I would choose to believe a student over a longtime colleague and friend."

The skin of her jaw stung.

Warren's face softened, pleased with himself. "I might even speculate that there were elements of fantasy on the girl's part. You know these kids. It's all sex."

She recalled Julie's silver-tipped fingers dropping trail mix into Christophe's hand, and E.J. and Larissa pouring themselves toward each other. Warren was right, except the attraction didn't leap naturally upwards over a hurdle of a decade or more. Something happened in those intervening years, more than the tug of gravity, the loss of hair, the padding of throat and waist, something that shriveled and distorted those young, passionate currents that surged between attraction, repulsion, and convergence into what was operating in this room.

"This isn't personal, Warren," she answered, managing to keep her voice even.

"Of course not. I'm not suggesting that," he said smoothly, and she realized that he, the others, too, thought she and Mel had been lovers, and that he had spurned her. No one looked at her. They were shuffling their papers and nodding judiciously. If she'd been in the Resistance, she would blow up this room, but instead, she faced a life sentence of lunches with these people.

On Wednesday, at the end of class, Christophe waited for her, leaning against the slide projector cart until everyone else had left. He'd made a special effort at grooming, giving himself a new haircut—with gardening shears, by the look of it. Under his oversized military jacket, he was wearing an ugly tweed sports coat.

"Is this going to be an excuse about why you didn't have your work today?" Daveen asked, immediately ashamed that she sounded like her sixth-grade teacher. She forced herself to wait patiently as he searched through the pockets in his military jacket. He opened flaps, reached inside, then not finding what he wanted, dug into the pockets of his sports coat. She could feel her face hardening as he rechecked his pockets. Finally, he produced a thin wine-red book, his passport.

"I have been called back to France . . . " His voice caught. "To serve in the military. That is why I do not have my work. I have been trying to see if there is some way for me to postpone, but there is not." He shoved his passport back into a pocket, and shifted his weight.

She asked if he had to leave immediately, in the middle of the term, imagining his bad hair sticking out from beneath a natty Foreign Legion cap.

"There is no other way. I have checked. But I am hoping that you will do me a favor."

"Sure." She doubted a few sentences to his draft board in her French would help.

He pointed to a tripod resting in a corner of the room, beside it a camera bag. "Would you take a photograph of me, here in this classroom?"

She hadn't taken a picture since last summer and didn't want to fumble in front of a student. And someone could come in and think he was her pet. Like Mel. "I don't think–"

"The time it will not take much. My camera is ready, see." He opened his bag and pulled out an old twin-lens Rollei, like one she'd once owned. "I have it in my mind. All I need is you to focus and release the shutter," he said, hurrying to the tripod and attaching the camera.

She watched him rush to position a chair in front of the chalkboard, eager to convince her. Her notes on the Kelvin scale, loopy as Arabic, would make a nice background.

"If this won't take too long," she said, flattered that he wanted a souvenir from her class. She bent to look into the camera.

"Wait," he said. He struggled out of his military jacket, adjusted his tweed jacket, then sat down and crossed and re-crossed his legs. "How does this look?"

Through the ground glass, his face seemed to balloon toward her. She remembered what she'd said earlier about the dance between the photographer and subject and imagined her left hand on his shoulder, her right hand in his. She turned the focus knob back and forth, forcing his image to blur, then snap into clarity. In the magnifying screen, she noticed that where his left eyebrow sloped outward, the individual hairs smoothed to a central line, like the vane of a feather, she could feel her fingertip touch that black point. Repositioning the lens, she focused again—he still seemed too close—but she kept her eye to the ground glass and asked if he was ready. He straightened his shoulders, placed both feet squarely on the floor, and lifted his chin, like the perfect nineteenth century gentleman. Then his eyes narrowed in an expression she couldn't decipher, embarrassment, amusement, she couldn't tell.

Releasing the shutter, she realized that she'd been holding her breath. She looked up across a distance that seemed to have shrunk. Her voice sounded too loud when she said, "There are still several frames left on the roll. Would you like me to finish the roll off?"

"Thank you, no. I have something else in mind." His tone was clipped, as if he had no further use for her. He stood and walked to her side. Wishing she hadn't cooperated, she shook his hand.

"Will you be in class next week?" she asked, smiled evenly.

"No. I must leave this weekend."

At least she wouldn't have to see him again. "Good luck to you then."

Several weeks later, on the last day before spring break, Daveen tiptoed her way through a sea of bodies lolling on the lawn in front of the Art Building. Drawn outdoors by the unseasonal warmth, the students drowsed, limbs entwined, not stirring as she stepped over them, except to scowl when her shadow interrupted the sun. She kept her eyes lifted, pretending to study the pediment's bas-relief where a bearded figure in a toga lectured to a small circle of students, faces lifted in rapt awe. Irony was unusual in neo-classical art.

In the Art Department office, Chuck was checking his mail. With a nod, which meant that he was too occupied to answer her hello, he moved aside. She didn't have to keep this up, she thought, reaching into her mailbox. In five weeks when the term was over, she could quit, open a studio, go into business for herself. PR photography would pay the bills until she developed something better. She tossed aside the flyers from art supply houses, saved the graduation notice—donning her robes and colors could be her last official duty if she decided to quit—and came to a large, plain envelope with foreign stamps and no return address. Her name and the college's address were written in a large, sprawling hand. Through the manila, she could feel nothing. She undid the metal brad and reached in. One thick sheet of paper. She pulled it out and turned it over.

It was a black and white photograh showing her classroom, the chalkboard covered with her notes in the background, track lights visible above. In the center, on one of the regulation molded plastic chairs, sat Christophe Artaud, naked. Confused, she stared at Christophe's long, pale body folded modestly, his hands in his lap hiding his genitals. He was in the exact position he'd struck for her a couple of weeks ago, legs crossed, shoulders straight, eyes directed at the lens, directed at her. Chuck brushed past her and she slid the picture back into the envelope, praying he hadn't seen it. She walked unsteadily to her office and shut the door carefully. Heart thumping, she pulled out the photograph again. A month ago, he'd been dressed, she was sure of that. She remembered the rumpled sports coat over his un-ironed, high-buttoned shirt. And heavy black shoes with thick white socks. One sock—the right one—had sagged around his ankle to expose an almost iridescent shin. She couldn't remember his trousers. In this image his bare feet glowed, narrow and delicate. She forced herself to take several long, deep breaths. She had not taken this photograph, she was sure of that. He must have stripped after she left the classroom and used a self-timer. But why? Was this intended to shock her? Embarrass her? Mock her? He'd gone back to France—she checked the stamps and postmark again—so why bother? Unless this was the opening gambit in a campaign of entrapment. Unless someone here had put him up to it. She thought of Mel.

She hadn't been to his office since the Mindy Ott business and had forgotten the stinging smell of oils and paint thinner. Through the window at the back of the painting studio, she saw him talking on the phone. He held up his palm, asking to her to wait, acting natural, as if it hadn't been years since the last time she'd come to see him. She glanced at the student canvases stacked along his office walls, terrible messes smeared with grays and browns in imitation of Francis Bacon and, angry though she was, felt a wash of sympathy for Mel.

When he finished, he swiveled to face her, grinning broadly. "I want to say thank you, Daveen. Yesterday I got a call from the Dean saying that the committee had recommended me. I know how you've felt about me, but the Dean said the recommendation came with unanimous support. Thank you for that." He rubbed his hand over his shaved head that looked not chic, but like a futile effort to hide hair loss. He used to remind her of the cute boy who sat in the back of her high school home room who could be counted on to unhinge the class; now he looked like he could be worried about mortgage rates. The skin beneath his eyes was wrinkled like deflated balloons. The current Mindy Otts must find him pathetic.

"I came to ask you what you make of this." She handed him Christophe's photograph.

"Student of yours?"

"Used to be in my Wednesday class. That's my room, but I hardly know him."

He squinted at the print, too vain, she guessed, to wear glasses. "I thought only girls did this kind of thing." She watched for a flicker of amusement or a sign that he'd seen it before. Nothing.

"I thought you might be able to illuminate this for me."

He shook his head. "No, I'm out of touch with student sexual ambitions. I've crossed to the other side, Daveen."

"What do you mean?"

He shrugged. "I'm no longer on the radar screen."

"Poor Mel," she said. "And I had hoped you'd be able to tell me what this was all about."

He handed back the picture and she pretended to study it, giving him a moment to take in what she was implying.

"You don't think I had anything to do with this, do you?" He propped his boot onto the wastebasket, feigning nonchalance. "Why would I?"

"I can think of several reasons."

"Like suspicions you've raised against me?"

So much for confidentiality on the tenure committee. "Mel, I just followed customary procedures."

"Ah, yes, Daveen, Miss Customary Procedures. Does this go on your vita before or after your Miss Morality title?" He produced an artificial smile.

She glared at him, stung, realizing how moments ago he'd acted as if he were genuinely glad to see her, not as if he wanted to sabotage her. She considered this. Why, indeed, would he? Now she wasn't sure. With his tenure being decided, he would be a fool to jeopardize his future with a prank that could unravel so easily. She averted her gaze, humiliated to realize that she'd been wrong. Christophe's gesture, whatever it meant, had nothing to do with Mel.

She forced a breath from her lungs, and said, "I'm sorry."

Mel snorted and dropped his foot from the wastebasket. His face was hard. "The thanks stands for making it unanimous. I know how that must have cost you your principles."

She stepped back, her foot catching on a row of canvases, and tried to grab them before they fell, crushing Christophe's picture. Shaken, trying to compose herself, she smoothed the rumpled surface and took in his now wrinkled face, which seemed to shift from a taunt to an invitation, as if he were toying with her. A puzzling sensation, wistfulness mingled with rebellion, spread through her chest. The longer she stared the more inscrutable his expression became until the detailed grays of the image dissolved and she was swimming backwards through them to the moment when she had taken the photograph, the other photograph, when he was clothed, and she had thought she was doing him a favor. But she was no longer looking at him, but trying to decipher what it was he had seen looking at her. Had he glimpsed a woman more interesting, more quixotic, more surprising than whom she knew herself to be? Not a washout, but someone reckless and alive, someone capable of being a partner in a dance. A collaborator, an unwitting collaborator perhaps, but still, a collaborator. The possibility of this, of being someone she didn't recognize exhilarated Daveen, and she laughed. And laughed.

Near Miss

A JACKAL WIND BLEW OUT of the west, rattling the leaky casements of Rolly's studio on the third floor of the Art Building. When a window banged open, he looked up from his worktable, pretending that his concentration had been broken though his struggle to say focused had been lost some time ago. Meg was grading papers on the couch, naked except for his old Cranbrooke sweatshirt she had donned after they'd made love.

"I'll get that," he said, setting down the razor and the willow sapling, glad to interrupt his endless silent review of conversations real and imagined in which he spelled out to his wife, Alice, why they shouldn't have a baby.

He wedged a rag in the window as he latched it, finding the grating of metal against metal a fit expression of his mood. Alice was two months pregnant. He returned his worktable and the dry paper cast he had molded onto a willow stalk. Picking up the razor, he slid the blade down the length of the cast, slicing it open.

He was working on an installation commissioned by a new sculpture museum in upstate New York. At this point in his career, ready to make his mark, he wanted to produce something exceptional, but Alice's pregnancy had almost derailed him. After a couple of false starts, he had decided to create a rootless, branchless forest from lightweight paper casts molded on thin branches he'd collected near the river.

Meg came up behind him and let her red hair fall in the light of his work lamp. "How much longer?"

"This is the last for now." He pried the thin shell from the sapling.

After Alice told him she was pregnant, he'd tried to break it off with Meg, but couldn't. Even with the guilt, the whispered phone calls, the afternoons together in his studio, all the secrecy and subterfuge thrilled him almost as much as his direct physical longing for her. Meg made everything else possible. She lightened his life rather than complicated it.

Outside the window a large icicle cracked free from the gutter and fell, followed by a smattering of snow.

"Let me breathe you in for a minute."

She settled against him and held him close, her body narrow, almost bony beneath his sweatshirt. "It's getting late."

"It's okay. Alice works late on Tuesday. Can you stay, take a look at this with me?"

She glanced over his shoulder at the school clock. "For a little while."

"Good." He kissed her throat. "Can you give me a hand with these?" He pulled out some galvanized buckets half-filled with sand. "Let's line them up in the center, three straight rows, a foot apart."

A loose bundle of hollow casts he had made earlier stood at the end of his work bench. He handed one to Meg. "See if they'll stay more or less upright, one in each bucket. Sort of shove them down, like this." He pressed one into the sand and it swayed slightly, a denuded ghost tree.

Together they placed one cast in each bucket until three rows of ten stood in the center of the studio, as orderly and surreal as a machine planted forest. Even with the background mess of easels, sawhorses, drawings taped to the walls, the papery white forms, slender and pure, asserted a powerful presence.

Excited, Rolly sighted down the center row. "So what do you think?"

"They look sad, and elegant. A regiment of husks abandoned. Formerly living."

"This is just to get an idea. I'm thinking about a very tight arrangement, a grid of one hundred of these." He righted one of the casts that tipped. "Ten rows of ten, not grounded like these, but suspended by narrow—I hope invisible—wires to hang a couple of feet above the floor.

"God, this is better than what I hoped for." He walked to Meg's side and propped his chin on her head, half-worrying that this was coming together too easily. Nothing ever came out quite the way he planned, but this unaccountable leap between conception and form was the great reward for him in making art.

"I can see it now, a retrospective at the Whitney, a Guggenheim fellowship, a monograph—" She broke off at the sound of the phone.

Rolly reached for receiver above his worktable, annoyed. "Yes."

"Can you come home?" It was Alice.

He gave Meg a warning look. "I'm busy working. Where are you?" He could hear Alice breathing. In the middle of the arrangement of paper casts, one slipped in its sand foundation and sagged against another.

"I left work early. I want you to come home now. I don't feel good."

"I'm really involved here. How important is this?" He made a face as Meg picked up her clothes.

Alice's voice sounded tight. "I'm OK, but I want you to come home. I called the doctor."

"The doctor?"

"Just come home, please, as soon as you can."

"I'm on my way."

After he hung up, Meg asked, "What is it?"

"She wouldn't say. Can you have morning sickness in the afternoon?"

Meg shook her head. She had no children. "You go. I'll turn out the lights. Call me later if you can."

"I'll try."

He gunned the car out of the parking lot, wishing that he knew something about the intricacies of pregnancy. A month ago, Dr. Bersalt had talked generally about what was coming, week nine, week ten, week eleven, as if pregnancy were a ski course, the weeks slalom gates Alice would career through, flags snapping merrily, crowd cheering, Dr. Bersalt himself beaming, clocking the run. No mention of problems.

From the corner of their street, his and Alice's house looked dark, except for their bedroom window.

"Alice." No answer. He looked down the hall. In the dark kitchen the stove's light outlined a cup with a tea bag tag hanging out. He took the stairs three at a time.

She was in bed, obviously awake, but not opening her eyes. He tossed his jacket onto the rocking chair and lowered his weight onto the bed.

After a moment she blinked.

"Are you okay?" he asked.

She struggled to sit up, her fine, blonde hair flying away from her head in a static electricity halo as she pressed herself up against the headboard. Afraid to say anything, Rolly looked at her fingers curled on the edge of the sheet, then placed his hand on hers.

"This afternoon when I got home from the office, I thought my period had started." She withdrew her hand from his grasp. "But I'm not supposed to have a period. I called Dr. Bersalt and he said. . ." She stared at a point somewhere over Rolly's shoulder. "It's called breakthrough bleeding. I should take it easy."

"And?"

"Rest but not worry."

He picked up a pregnancy book on the bedside table.

She went on. "It says if the bleeding goes beyond spotting, if real bleeding starts, there's a chance—it says a chance—of a miscarriage."

He put down the book and drew her to him, seeing a way out, then immediately regretting it. He stroked her back, but she held herself rigid, resisting comfort.

"But that also means that most of the time it doesn't happen, right? Everything's okay," he said.

She didn't say anything.

"Is there anything we're supposed to do?"

"Wait."

"That's it?"

"If there's a change, call him."

"That's it?"

She nodded.

"Okay, I'll wait."

He drove to the mall for take-out pizza. Amid the jangle of shouted orders, he thought about calling Meg. He wouldn't tell her about Alice, that she was scared and bleeding, that he didn't know what to do. He just wanted to hear that little catching sound she made at the end of some of her words. In the studio, he had begged her to say words that end in 'g,' just so he could hear that snag. "Shoppin-ga, washin-ga, holdin-ga," she'd offered and he had said, "How about dancin-ga, kissin-ga, love-makin-ga?" He imagined her picking up the phone and saying "hello." He couldn't imagine what he would say.

It began to snow. Tiny flakes mounded at the edge of the windshield by the time he got home.

They ate in bed, watching a movie. After a few bites, Alice put her pizza aside and nestled close to him. He lowered the volume as guys in black commando suits took over a space ship. Against the sound of explosions no louder than a cap gun's, he listened to Alice breathe and tried to follow the near miss on the end of the world.

A month ago, when he had told Meg about the baby, she had held his head against her chest and whispered, "It's okay, Rolly." He had believed her. Beside him, Alice slept, without defense. He lay down, resting his hand on her belly.

It was still dark outside when he awoke, and Alice's weight beside him was missing. He swung his feet to the floor and listened. The snow had stopped. Beyond the bedroom door the hall was completely dark. After a moment he could see that the bathroom door was closed. Frightened, he stood.

"Alice," he whispered. From inside he heard a low sound. "Can I come in?"

"No."

He opened the door. She was bent over on the toilet. In the faint light from the window, her back glowed with the sickly iridescence of a fish curling on ice. He knelt beside her, lifting the sweaty hair that clung to her neck. Beyond the unshuttered half of the window, the clouds had broken apart and were streaking across the moon.

"I'll call the doctor."

"No." Her lunar face floated near his hand. "I don't want to bother him. It's too late."

"I'm calling him."

"Rolly—" She made a gasping sound. "I think I better go to the hospital."

He called Dr. Bersalt's service, dressed, started the car and left it running while he gathered her robe, her coat and boots. Upstairs again, he turned on the hall light and saw Alice still hunched over on the toilet. The tile floor was smeared pink where she'd tried to clean up blood. He forced himself to look calm as she stood and he wrapped her robe around her. Over her shoulder he saw that the toilet water was scarlet.

Fingers clumsy, he worked at the buttons of her coat, finally managing to shove the top one through. With his arm around her shoulders, he held her upright as she put her feet in her boots, first the right, then the left, toes pointed like a dancer's. Drops of blood speckled her feet. He closed his eyes and held her close.

"I've got to get towels," she said, pulling away. "For in the car." Her teeth were chattering.

"I've got them," he said.

The hospital door sprang open at his touch. Alice flinched, tucking into his side. In front of them a sea of shining linoleum stretched in all directions. Across the empty space, behind glass, he saw a white-hatted nurse. Alice started to keel over, but he held tight, guiding her forward across the slick floor, fighting the urge to sprint to the nurse. When they reached the window, Alice put her hand on the glass to steady herself, her fingers fitting into the circle of a NO SMOKING sign, and the nurse's glasses turned in their direction.

"If you'll fill out these . . ." She slid papers through the opening, then stopped, squinting to focus her eyes on something behind them. Rolly turned and saw animal tracks, spatters of blood smeared by Alice's boots.

A couple of men in blue hospital fatigues appeared. Alice swayed forward into their arms and they led her through swinging metal doors.

"Where are you going?" Rolly's voice boomed through the quiet hall as he trailed them.

The taller guy said, "If you'll just take a seat, sir."

"It's okay, Rolly. I'm okay," Alice called out, looking back.

"No. Wait."

A couple of orderlies he hadn't seen stepped close. "Hey, man, be cool. They're just taking her in. They got a job to do, see."

"Take your hands off me." Rolly twisted, ready to strike.

"We're not touching you, man. Take it easy."

Rolly refused their offer of coffee. He tried to imagine what was happening to her now, but old images flooded his mind, close-up details: the triangular scar on her forearm from the iron, her hands folding a napkin, in the car, sunlight sliding over her jaw and shoulder, the way her lips tensed when she was in pain.

Someone, one of the orderlies, tapped his arm. "Doc says come in now."

Alice lay on the gurney wrapped in a thick white blanket, her arms on top, her shoulders covered by a pale blue gown, her face flattened with fright. He tried to touch her, but a nurse stepped between them.

"Mr. Becotte." Rolly turned. A man in blue scrubs introduced himself and said this wasn't a crisis but that they were going to have to proceed.

The words were coming too fast. Rolly could pick out single words—

hemorrhaging . . . dilation . . . tissue . . . infection—but he couldn't make out their meaning. He inched toward Alice, but was held back by a nurse maneuvering an IV stand.

". . . spontaneous abortion . . ."

Something feral scurried in the hollow dark of his skull.

He heard Alice gasp, "Stop."

"What are you doing?" he demanded.

"We have to take this off before surgery." A nurse tugged at Alice's wedding band.

"It doesn't come off." Alice tightened her hand into a fist. "I won't lose it. I promise."

The older nurse bent down. "It's all right, dear. We'll put tape over it. Everything will be fine." She nodded as others began to wheel the gurney toward double doors.

"Rolly?"

"I'm right here." He pushed between the nurses.

"Am I going to die?"

"You are not going to die. The doctor said everything will be fine. I love you."

"The baby?"

He shook his head. No baby, tissue.

She stared at him, uncomprehending, and the nurses closed around her, nudging him aside.

❖

After the surgery, nurses settled Alice in for the night, and he sat with her, holding her hand, her wedding ring bundled in tape. She looked washed clean of feeling. When she said she wanted to sleep, he was relieved and walked out to their car, the sky still dark.

The streets were empty. Rounding the corner to their block, he saw yellow light spilling down their front steps. Burglarized? He wrestled the car door open and hurried toward the stairs. Through the open door, he saw their coat-tree holding Alice's plaid scarf. Slowly, quietly he walked upstairs. Bedclothes had been tossed to the floor, drawers spilled open, bloody footprints and wide red smears covered the bathroom floor. But nothing was missing. This was, he realized, how they had left it. He walked downstairs and closed the front door, disappointed. He wanted to catch an intruder. He wanted to have a reason to beat someone senseless. In the linen closet he found some old towels and a bucket. In the bathroom he filled the bucket. On his hands and knees he wiped the floor, red streaks turning pink, then fainter pink, until all that he could see on the shining tile was his own wet shadow.

At first light he returned to the hospital carrying a garish supermarket bouquet, the only flowers he could find at that hour. Alice was sitting up, pale, hair brushed flat, curls gone. Dr. Bersalt stood by her bed, his smooth eyebrows drawn together in a look Rolly guessed he'd practiced in front of a mirror. He nodded at Rolly.

"I know how hard this is for you, for you both, but first trimester miscarriages are quite common, more than you'd guess. They're nature's way of eliminating unsound fetuses."

Unsound. The other doctor had said tissue.

"These pregnancies would only yield babies with horrible defects."

Alice looked at Rolly and tightened her grip on his hand. He was grateful, for what, he wasn't sure: for her love? for relief at a monster baby not born? for the justice of being punished for Meg?

Alice left the hospital late that afternoon. For the next few days, they stayed home together, and he tried to think of ways to please her. He fixed all their meals, read to her from the paper, bought her a green sweater with short sleeves for spring. He taught his classes but avoided his studio. Meg left several messages on his voicemail at the office, but he erased them. He tried not to think about her, but as he drifted off to sleep holding Alice, some memory would ambush him, the weight of her against his chest or her pin-prick freckles, like flecks of rust, and he would wake, torn between self-loathing and longing.

After a week at home, he went back to the college. In less than a week his studio had become unfamiliar. The paper casts of branches that he'd left standing in the center of the floor looked like window display props, worse, like mall art. How had he fooled himself into thinking this trash had any value? Humiliation rippled over his skin. He'd been deluded in his happy-time fog with Meg.

He gathered the casts and flung them in a heap in the corner. Turning away, he sat on a stool next to a crate that held the samples of rare woods—ebony, Madagascar mahogany, tiger maple, Sacred Heart—he'd collected for sculptural canoes he planned, but hadn't begun. Picking up a curled section of basswood bark, he envisioned a river in misty morning light, its surface peeling open as a blade-thin boat rose up, and kept rising, cataracts of water swirling away until blackness blotted out everything else. Canoes, mythic canoes, vessels for journeying, all passage, no end, the ancient quest revisited, that's what he would create.

Feeling a surge of excitement, he pulled open a drawer, hunting for a pen and sketchbook, and found Meg's photograph, the one she'd given him when he said he couldn't remember exactly what she looked like when they were apart. She grinned, her freckled face tipped up. He started to put it back, then propped it on an empty coffee can.

❖

A few weeks later, after his 3-D design class, he heard a quick tapping on his studio door. Meg. Alternating waves of elation and dread took away his voice, but he stepped aside, inviting her in.

She walked past him, threw her coat on the couch, then knelt beside the small canoe, tucking her skirt under her knees to avoid the pile of stones. This canoe, which he'd been working on, was coated with an opaque gray polymer that gleamed pewter and left the textural burrs shining like scars. Inside, the hull was lined with black-dyed fur that drank light so completely the interior seemed to throb. Meg lowered her hand into the fur.

"Something new?" she asked.

"All of a sudden, some ideas hit me," he said, grateful for neutral ground. "Awhile back I'd thought about building some mythic canoes, but I didn't know where to go then."

"Is that why I haven't heard from you?" She turned to face him.

He looked for signs of accusation, but her candy-blue eyes were clear.

"It's not that. It's . . . "

"Alice," she guessed.

"Yes."

"Did you tell her about us?"

He shook his head, aware of a new silence in the room. He had just rejected the acceptable explanation, the one she'd come prepared to hear. She looked down at the pile of stones, nudged one with her foot.

He scrambled, searching for something to say to make what he'd said come out differently as he walked to her side. From beneath the canoe, he lifted a stone he'd wrapped in black rice paper and lashed with scarlet twine. "These are going to be cargo for the canoes. I'm wrapping them. Here's one." He held it out to her, wanting her to take it, to feel its weight as a testament of his regret.

She turned it over and handed it back. He wanted to say he was sorry, that he loved her. Instead he said, "These will be funereal canoes, a flotilla of them, which will carry souls." He glanced at the wrapped stone he held.

She stood up and walked toward his workbench. "What's that supposed to mean?"

"Didn't Freud say that we all have two basic urges? One, for generation, *libido*, you and I know about that." He was a wind-up professor toy, talking too fast. Her eyes narrowed, but he couldn't stop himself. "The other, *thanatos*, the desire to return to the state of the stone."

"Is that what you want? To become a stone?"

He dropped it into the fur. The canoe wobbled, and he stilled it with his foot. "Alice had a miscarriage."

Her features drew together slowly, like a knot being tightened, as she took in what he'd said, then softened. "How awful." She walked toward him and set her cheek against his chest.

A sense of gratitude, almost an ache, welled up inside him. He had forgotten how her touch made him feel.

"I love you, Rolly."

"I thought I could hold it all together, but in the hospital . . . it wasn't the baby's dying, but it was me tearing out her insides, even though she doesn't know it. It was me, you and me."

She jerked away as if he'd hit her, but he went on. "I can't do this. Please. I don't know what comes next."

She glared at him, shoving aside his hand as he reached for her. "Get the hell away. I'm sorry, but the miscarriage didn't happen because of you, or because of you and me. You say you loved me." She swallowed, turned away, then back, fighting tears. "We carved out a space for ourselves, something real, something genuine and deep. Doesn't that matter to you?"

"Oh, Meg, please."

"Please what? Make it easy for you?"

He looked down at the canoe at his feet, as she growled, "Go to hell," and strode out, leaving a vacuum.

Holding still, he listened to waves of students pass in the corridor outside his door. When that faded, he surveyed the studio, the drawings taped to the walls, his abandoned tree casts, and the two small canoes at his feet, the best work he'd ever produced. Revulsion seeped through him. He reached for the nearby stool and smashed it down on the nearest canoe, then grabbed its broken stempiece and whirled what held together above his head, then let it fly. It crashed above the tree casts, dark pieces dropping among the white hollow husks, wavering and collapsing, and Rolly holding his breath, waiting for the next thing to happen.

A Paris Story

KLINE WAS FIFTY-EIGHT, FOURTEEN YEARS older than she. Now that they were both middle-aged, Suzanna thought the difference wouldn't seem so great. A year ago he had called and waited for her to know his voice, but she hadn't. Sixteen years it had been. He had found a snapshot of them together, a picnic on the beach. She remembered the moment. Kline's head was in her lap and he was squinting at his friend—what was his name?—who held the camera. Hair whipping in her face, her mouth open in a laugh. She looked so inconsequential, not the way she had felt, not powerfully in love.

What do you look like now? he had asked. My face is thinner, my hair longer. Some gray, some lines, no glasses yet. She was being modest. The doughy, Irish features in the snapshot had sharpened into prettiness. And you, she had asked, what do you look like, still handsome? You would recognize me. And she imagined his uncanny blue eyes under sagging lids, his hair thick and gray. Deep lines, maybe folds, would frame his mouth.

Do you ever think of me? he had asked, and Suzanna had laughed. No, not really, not in years. And you? All the time. She had felt elated.

Do you ever come to Washington? he had asked.

❖

"Suzanna."

Kline came up behind her in the hotel lobby. "You haven't changed at all."

He was taller than she remembered, a little stooped, still disarmingly handsome. His chin was knobbier than she remembered, with tiny soft pouches of flesh on either side, but his eyes were as blue as ever.

After a quick scan of her face, no more than an acknowledgment, he turned away and looked around the glittering atrium at the crowd of conventioneers. "A drink, then?" he asked.

She had imagined him telling her how wonderful she looked. His eyes were supposed to examine her face, register, then appreciate the freckles that had appeared in the past few years, the now definite planes of her cheeks, even the lines around her eyes. For Kline to really take her in, to acknowledge that she was now strong and capable, was why she had come, she now realized. Until this moment, she thought she was just curious.

Kline squeezed her elbow as he steered them around clusters of mauve barrel chairs toward a table umbrella-ed by a large palm strung with lights. He apologized for being late. Traffic was bad. "I remember, though, you were always late."

"Was I? I don't remember that. Perhaps you're thinking of someone else." Suzanna answered, amused.

"No. I remember everything about you exactly." He lifted her coat and draped it over a chair.

"I have changed then." She sank into one of the fat chairs and smiled up at him. "I like being early now. I don't mind waiting."

Kline glanced at her as he sat down. "Have you? Changed, that is? I wonder. I think I depend on your not changing."

"Then prepare to be disappointed."

"By you? Never."

Her heart made a strange, uncomfortable leap. "Why did you contact me, after so long?"

He inhaled deeply and held the breath. "Because, in a way, you've never left me."

"I left you?"

"Yes, you left. But now, I find it hard knowing where to start."

"Not too hard," she answered. "There's what I'm doing now and what you're doing now. There's what we've done for the past ten, fifteen years. There's—"

"Suzanna." He leaned forward, resting his arms on his knees, hands clasped, inches from where her skirt fell away from her crossed legs. "Things have changed since I called. Now, I want to tell you a story. I want this story to be inside you before we go on, but it's risky, this story. You see, I don't know how it will end. I don't even know what it means, to me that is. So I don't know what you will see, what you may understand or come to believe about me that I don't yet know myself."

He straightened and unwound the purple scarf around his neck. The soft wool fell away and she saw his skin scraped red from a rough shave, with a few un-cropped hairs along the jaw line. She had forgotten how beautiful she found his neck, how its slopes and hollows called out to her tongue.

She looked away. Kline ordered drinks, then turned back to Suzanna. "You do see the risk, don't you? I don't want to shrink in your view."

She was flattered. "There may be risks for me, too, in your story. I can fail to understand, magnify or dismiss, take the wrong slant." She stopped, realizing that she might. She didn't want this to happen. Above all, she wanted to impress him. She wanted him to understand how much she had grown since they had broken up, how mature she now was, no longer shattered, not the wailing woman holding out long strands of someone else's blonde hair found in their bed.

"Tell me the story," she said.

He smiled, relieved, and settled back into the chair. "I'm not going to tell you the story straight out. I'm going to divide it into chapters."

"Oh, good," she said, gratified that he had designed an entertainment for her.

"This story is set in Paris. That's where I was last month when your letter arrived. That's why I didn't call right away. I was there for three weeks, filming a documentary for television, advances in waste management, the scenic side of garbage. Anyway, I stayed in the apartment of friends, a large place, half a city block. I was made to feel as if it were mine. Each night the maid polished my shoes and laundered my shirts, and we, Isabelle and Lucien, never got in each other's way. We seldom saw one another until dinner, which was always formal, served by a maid. Not my usual style." He picked up the glass the waitress had set on the table and smiled up at Suzanna.

His style, as she had known it the five years they were together, eclipsed domesticity. Before she had seen his apartment, he had told her he could kick a soccer ball in his living room and not break anything. What about the windows, she had wanted to ask, but hadn't. After she moved in and then out five years later with her few pieces of Bauhaus furniture, she came back to that image of Kline in a vacant white space, soccer balls rocketing around him. Parisian elegance didn't fit. "No. Not you at all, but wonderfully decadent."

"Yes, wonderfully. I think I could compromise myself and live like that." He grinned.

She felt completely at ease, happy, as if the years had actually allowed her to catch up to Kline.

"Chapter One. One evening Lucien said that he had invited a woman, an old friend of his and Isabelle's, to dinner. This was not, he explained, any kind of a fix-up or date. No, she, this woman, Claire, was having a bad time, and he thought an evening with friends and with me, an interesting American, might pick her up. A few days earlier this Claire had been told by her husband that he loved another woman. He, Claire's husband, had decided that he should move in with his lover for three weeks, then move back in with Claire, his wife, for three weeks, and after that decide with whom he should live."

"That's intolerable," Suzanna snapped. "I would never—"

Kline leaned forward and brushed her knee. "No, you wouldn't. I know that . . . "

Suzanna had the impression that he saw this as some kind of limitation on her part.

He went on. "That first evening we all talked in the living room, I saw none of the agitation that Isabelle and Lucien had described, nor the kind of impervious heroics I can see you mustering." He took Suzanna's drink from her hand and set it down on the small table, then threaded his fingers through hers, as if he had read her thoughts and wanted to dispel them. "She looked nice, nothing special, maybe a little distracted, but a good guest, helping the conversation."

Kline told about the dinner, how Lucien and Isabelle had been light and witty, but also solicitous, very kind. Suzanna imagined candlelight, the tinkle of wine glasses, rustling French murmurs. This woman, Claire,

Kline said, began telling them of a phone call with her husband that day and in a moment she was crying. When she was through, she had looked at Isabelle and said she was miserable and didn't know what to do. Isabelle had then turned to Kline and asked, "What should she do, Kline?"

Kline squeezed Suzanna's hand. "They all looked at me. I felt I must reward their confidence, their trust in me. I must prove that their friendship with me was not misplaced."

"What did you say?" Suzanna felt put on the spot herself, doubting she would have answered well, but sure he had.

Kline answered in a soft, almost swaying cadence, and Suzanna knew that this rhythm was how he must have spoken to this French woman, knew he had relied on gentle inflection to bridge any gap of comprehension, of language or experience, like talking to a child. She felt cut out.

"I told her, Claire, that she should call her husband's girlfriend and set up an appointment to meet alone. Insist that it be soon. When they were together, she should say that she wants the girlfriend to tell her about the happiest time she has ever had with her husband. She must say that, much as hearing this will hurt her, Claire, she must know this so that she can determine where her husband belongs, whether she should fight for him or not."

This was exactly right, the best thing that could be done. How did Kline always do this, discover an unimaginably inventive, yet perfect purchase on events? When they had been together, she had been awed by him always. Again, his insight and invention were marvelous to her. She pressed his hand in delight.

"What did she say, this Claire?"

"She clapped her hands, just once, and said, 'That's it. That I must do. Thank you.' "

Suzanna waited for more, but Kline withdrew his hand from hers and took a sip of his drink. "And then?" she asked.

"That was all. Isabelle and Lucien seemed to be quarreling silently, having to do, it seemed, with what I had said, or maybe with Claire. Her husband, you see, is also a friend of theirs. But that was all. End of Chapter One."

He turned away to signal the waitress, and it came to Suzanna that as he was telling the story he had not once looked at her. He had gazed at her hands, over her shoulder at the silent piano, but not at her. She wondered if he regretted calling her a year ago, then setting up this evening. Perhaps he had come this far based on a memory, but now, in her presence, he was disconcerted, even disappointed. She wondered how his version of her had changed since they had been together, what had she become for him? She knew what he had become for her: the man who had taught her to be a woman, that's how she thought of him, the man who had forced her to define herself.

She looked across at him and found him studying her intently, as he had not done earlier. Glad, relieved, she smiled.

"Chapter Two?" she asked, wanting to keep him looking at her. "Do I get Chapter Two?"

"Oh, yes. Of course. Two days later, Isabelle asked me if Claire could come visit me on the shoot. Isabelle thought Claire needed a diversion. Watching a film crew for a few hours, which would be a great pleasure. She said Claire had told her she enjoyed my company.

"She arrived after we'd begun setting up. We were filming in the yard of a paper mill, along a canal, interviewing workers. She stayed out of the way, very polite, a schoolgirl on a field trip. At the end of the day, she was still there. She asked if I wanted a ride, a tour, of her Paris. Little squares, neighborhoods I might never have seen on the Right Bank, ancient saddle makers, funny signs, neon pipes and vests, a bakery producing only meringues, that sort of thing. Favorites of hers. Can you imagine?"

She could. She'd been to Paris many times, but now she imagined a movie Paris, black and white, seen from a fast sports car, with tilting buildings, flashes of sky, a jazz horn sound track. She felt edgy and excited, guessing this was how Kline must have felt. The surprise of it, for him, a filmmaker, seeing the real thing, a cinematic Paris.

He went on. "Afterwards, she stopped in front of Lucien and Isabelle's and I got out. I wanted to give her something. There were no flower vendors nearby. In my pocket I found a scarf, green paisley, I'd bought when I arrived and hadn't used. I handed it to her and she kissed my palm, pressing my hand to her lips longer than . . . I was so surprised. I was embarrassed for her really." He stopped speaking and stared at Suzanna carefully. "End of Chapter Two."

He stretched his legs, bringing his shoes to rest on the base of Suzanna's chair and waited, a silence opening around them.

"I'm worried," she said.

"Yes?" He pushed aside the glasses on the table between them. "About what?

"About Claire."

He broke out in a laugh. "What about me? Why aren't you worried about me?"

"You? Nothing can happen to you. But this Claire, she's a wobbly gyroscope."

Kline leaned closer and touched her cheek. "You think that, do you? How very strange you are."

Pleased to have the power to surprise him, she said nothing, simply held his gaze. He kissed her, a small kiss, then said, "Let's go to dinner."

The cab left them in a dark neighborhood of taverns and grated store-fronts. Arabesques of graffiti, defiant and indecipherable, embellished the plywood-covered windows of the apartment building across the street from the Ethiopian restaurant they entered. Kline's gaffer had recommended this place.

"Isn't it extraordinary that we should be so easy together?" she asked, after they ordered.

"This is just what I expected. We know each other." He held her hand as he said this.

They talked about their work, about old friends, how little the other had changed, and were struck by the trivial details they both recalled. To Suzanna it was like being in the easy center of their time together, after the exciting, anxious months at the beginning and before the bad days at the end. Three distinct periods: beginning, middle, and end. So it seemed after they broke up, when Suzanna had considered it, re-enacting scenes, changing lines, altering the entrances and exits, in her own mind a stage manager of a still vivid but recently closed production. Later she thought of herself as an archeologist, digging in the dried remains of the past, chipping away, weighing, labeling, putting her small discoveries into boxes. In the end she had formulated a conclusion that satisfied her, explained it all. She had needed to be important to Kline. And though she was important, Kline couldn't accept her needing to be. He wanted them to meet on a level above need, a rarefied plain where only positive attraction operated, not weakness. Now she could see how lovely this vision had been.

She felt very close to him, very safe as they held hands throughout dinner. The stew-like food, the scooping and dipping with bread, made this simple. When the waiter cleared the dishes and brought them steamed towels, Kline took both of her hands in his, squeezing them hard. "Do you want Chapter Three?"

"Yes, please, go on," she answered, but she had forgotten he had a story other than the one between the two of them.

"The next evening we went out to dinner. I wasn't interested in her as a woman, but she seemed very nice, and we were both alone. Dinner was not good. She cried. She hadn't called her husband's girlfriend. She was frightened. Her pain engulfed me. When I took her home, she invited me into her apartment. She pointed out her children's rooms, a boy seventeen, a girl twelve, and asked me into her bedroom. I thought she was afraid if we sat in the living room, her children might come in and see she'd been crying. A large bed, low to the floor, covered with pillows, there was no other place to sit. She disappeared for a moment, then came back in dressed in an old bathrobe, terry cloth, you know, snagged and worn, her makeup gone, and she asked me to make love to her." Kline paused, narrowing his eyes as if he were focusing his thoughts. "But I couldn't let her make love to me."

Suzanna thought she must have missed something, that she hadn't heard correctly. "What do you mean?"

"Do you realize the risk I am taking?"

"In telling me?"

"Yes."

"Yes, I understand," she said, though she knew she didn't. "Now I'm worried about you."

Kline rose and embraced her. "Oh, my god," he said, brushing her hair away from her face. "Let's go."

When they arrived at his townhouse, Kline put on a CD and went in search of brandy. The sounds of rustling grasses, wind, animals scurrying, the high keening notes of a violin filled the room. Suzanna took in the expensive, worn furniture, the general air of disarray. He still wedged unanswered letters between his shelved books where they stood out like white and yellow flags. You would recognize me, he had said. The old yearning for him flared inside her.

Her throat went dry at the sight of him coming from the dark hall.

"It looks like you had an affair with an interior decorator. Did you break up before she convinced you to get fancy Italian lamps?" she asked, as he handed her a brandy. She tucked her legs beneath her and turned to him as he sat beside her.

"It's not that bad, is it?" Kline looked around the room as if he hadn't noticed it for some time. "It is awful. But you do like those lights, don't you?" indicating the studio spotlights that cast faint beams of light, like sails, across the ceiling.

"Very nice. Like you," Suzanna answered, taking a sip, wondering if they would make love.

His hand rested on her shoulder. He lifted her hair, then let in drop in waves. Neither spoke.

"Is it time?" she asked, resting her head along the back of the couch, just touching his arm. "For your story, I mean. Chapter Four." She wanted to hurry the story along, to get rid of the French woman.

"You want to hear it?"

She nodded yes, uncertain, but wanting to prove herself capacious and wise.

"The next day I decided that this was all wrong, that she needed me as a defense or a ploy against her husband, and that if I were absent, she could act more directly, that this would be better. So I didn't call her, though I knew she expected me to. I worked late at the studio, screening rushes. When I came out, it was well after midnight. Her car was at the curb. I don't know how long she was there. She called to me, said she wanted to take me out. I hesitated. 'Oh, Kline, please,' she said in that sweet accent. Absolutely without guile, so ready to be hurt, yet risking it. Of course I went."

Why was he telling her this? His story no longer seemed like a gambit to amuse or entice her. Was it a test, of her perception or insight? Was this supposed to be a warning to her that he was taken, or was it a healing confession for him? Before she could begin to unravel these questions, he was telling her about a party they had gone to. On the way Claire asked him to flirt with other women, that she wanted to see how he looked with other women. He obliged. Now and then he would approach Claire and she was cool, indifferent. She left the party early with a man, a stranger he thought. Kline was surprised by how wounded he felt.

The night before Kline was to leave Paris, Lucien and Isabelle arranged a small dinner party. Kline asked if they would invite Claire. He had to find out why she had treated him so badly. She came. She was beautifully dressed, scented, made-up, more than he had ever seen her. At the door she threw her arms around him. She asked if he found her pretty, if he liked her dress. When he told her the dress made her look wealthy and uninteresting, but her brooch was lovely, she beamed. Beamed, Kline repeated, with an inward smile. Suzanna felt jealous and dismissed.

At the end of the evening, after the other guests had left, Claire, Kline, Lucien, and Isabelle had sat together dissecting the evening. A subdued dinner; there was little to say. Finally, Kline asked Claire why she had left him at the party, gone off with another man. She didn't answer.

Kline shook his head as if he were trying to dislodge the memory, then lifted his eyes to Suzanna. "Can you imagine how I felt?"

She could, in spite her jealousy. She took his hand and pressed it to her lips.

Kline's eyes were on Suzanna, but she could tell he was back in Paris, reenacting the scene. " 'I was so confused.' That was what Claire said."

"That bitch," Suzanna squeezed his hand, furious. "I would have slapped her. That makes me sick."

"You understand, don't you? You know what I was experiencing." He pulled Suzanna to him, settling her head against his shoulder, holding her tight.

She relaxed against his chest, pleased, but found that her memory of his long bones and muscles, even his scent, didn't correspond with what she now felt, a slackness, in his embrace.

"What did you do, when Claire said she was confused?" Suzanna asked, apprehensive. She shifted to see his face, but he was looking into the shadows.

"I felt sick, actually nauseous. Isabelle spoke up, accusing Claire of acting like a teenager. I left them and went to my room. Later, I don't know how long, there was a knock on my door. I thought it was either Lucien or Isabelle, but Claire came in. She asked me to take her home. I said no. But then, the next day I was leaving and would never see her again, so I went."

Suzanna wished she were sitting at the other end of the couch or in one of the opposite chairs, but moving would be too much of a gesture, of distancing, of rejection. What Suzanna required of herself, what she wanted to prove, was that she was capable of accepting what Kline was offering, though she had no idea what that was. She stirred and said, "I think you are crazy."

Kline laughed and kissed the top of her head. "I know you do, but are you still with me?"

She was.

From outside came the sound of voices. A car door slammed, then another, but inside it was silent. Suzanna wondered when the music had stopped.

"The next part is hard to explain. I don't understand it myself." He paused. "When we came to her building, I was determined not to go inside, but when she held my hand, I followed. I wasn't going to stay, but she took me into her bedroom and we made love."

Suzanna couldn't breathe. Why had she come? To prove that she had changed? To flirt? To see whether she might want to begin again, on different terms, her terms? She burned with embarrassment and shame.

"She's like a meteor. She's crashed into my life. I can't change it. Everything is different."

Suzanna looked at his hand resting on his thigh next to her. With one finger she stroked the back of his hand from wrist to the tip of his index finger. He had very graceful hands with squared-off nails, ridged like shells. She used to think, when she loved him, that his hands had an independent and unacknowledged life, loving things in a way that Kline didn't.

"She is going to destroy you," she said, resting her hand on his. Her hand was half the size of his.

"She might. But this may be the only chance I have to escape." He pulled his hand out from under hers. "I told Claire that if she left her husband, I would marry her." He draped his arm around Suzanna and drew her close. "I'm frightened," he whispered.

She wanted to save him. She kissed him. His mouth was startling, vast enough to lose herself in, and unknown, but as she held him, she could recognize the despair crouching in the bend of his neck, in the curve of his shoulder. She could feel him grow hard, before he pulled away and stared into space, as if straining to hear something very faint. Then his eyes shifted to her. He inclined his head, either giving up or giving in, she couldn't tell which, then struggled to his feet to dim the lamps.

The shadows that settled over the room obscured the details of Kline's life since they'd separated, making those years fold, like silk, into gauzy nothingness. Suzanna stood and slipped out of her clothes. Kline unbuttoned his shirt. They stood together and traced the slopes of each other's bodies. Her fingers followed the downward curves of his ribs and found the aging, inconsolable softness at his waist before they slid onto the couch.

As they moved together, she held back a part of herself to study him. Beneath her, he looked remote and disregarding as a statue. She wanted to reach down and touch his cheek, but stopped herself, not wanting to interrupt what seemed to be his private devotion. As the muscles of his abdomen and thighs flinched and gathered, she understood that he was, as always, lost to her. Forgiving him, still loving him, she withdrew all her claims.

Sunshine Every Day

THE ROOKWOOD IS A STATELY apartment building, built in the era between the First World War and the Great Depression, and occupied today by elderly couples and CFOs of established manufacturing firms. If, on a Monday morning, in the vast and echoing lobby you were to see a nattily dressed old man consult a scrap of paper for an apartment number, you would guess, rightly, that he was a real estate agent, an appraiser, or a moving company's agent, and you would also be right to surmise that property was about to change hands.

BERNARD STOOD OUTSIDE THE OPEN door of 14C, produced his card, and thought longingly of retiring to Seaside, as he smiled down at the tiny woman. What was her name? He ignored the Pomeranian growling behind her ankles, and waved his card in mid-air, pretending to check for smudges before handing it over, a practiced gesture he used to stretch out the first critical moments with a potential client. Proceeding slowly at the beginning was essential to success with the bereaved and the elderly. And god bless her, this woman was both. Recently widowed, she'd mentioned on the phone, and pushing eighty-five by the looks of her, with a wig the color of stewed apricots and a face the years had pummeled into submission. Giving Mrs. What's-her-name plenty of time to admire his suit, extra-starch shirt, no longer banker-short silver hair—that was a bad year—he lowered his eyes, imagining sun on his face, a breeze, being somewhere else. Her rat-faced puffball began to whine. Bernard glared down at the beast. Dogs, foul stenches, bickering relatives, these and worse he'd learned to accept. He noticed the carpet, an imitation Aubusson of the kind sold in shops connected to low-end casinos. This did not augur well. The dog ululated.

With a flourish, he gave his card to the old woman:

Bernard Doré
Appraisals. Ltd.
Paintings
Orientalia
Philately
Exonumia
Antiquities
Silver

Oh my goodness, thought Caroline, accepting the card. A gentleman of the old school. And such lovely hair, just like a symphony conductor's. Ronald would not like him one bit. Too smooth by half, he would say. But she didn't have to answer to Ronald any more. She fumbled for her glasses. It would serve him right if this fellow was a charlatan.

"Won't you come in?"

Bernard adjusted his grip on his briefcase, ready to swing at the yapping dog, and let the woman wave him into the high-ceilinged foyer. Her hands were unusually large-knuckled, her forearms crisscrossed with ropey veins. A countrywoman who'd come up in the world. He remembered her name: Mrs. Bledsoe, Mrs. Ronald Bledsoe.

He had been in so many apartments like this that even with his eyes closed he could find his way to the butler's pantry and pour himself a drink of water, which, in fact, he could use right now. The cramp behind his breastbone sent tentacles down his arm. He shouldn't have hurried. Willing the knot in his chest to subside, Bernard focused on business. Money here, the building said that, yet a rag on the floor. And an appalling settee against the opposite wall, a reproduction Biedermeier, no less.

Mrs. Bledsoe saw where he was looking. "My husband was the one who had the flair for taste."

Bernard tipped his head. "I would say he had quite a flair."

It was Philippe de Chalbert who'd taught Bernard that the elderly lose their aesthetic taste at the same moment they lose their taste buds, and in the same fashion, not in a general dulling of perception, but in sharply defined categories. With the tongue, the sensitivity to salt was the first to go. In the eye, it was color. "Just take me out back and shoot me, if I ever get to that state," Philippe had said, and Bernard, still a boy, had been amused and shocked.

"Would you mind taking off your shoes?" the woman said.

Bernard hid his annoyance as he untied his oxfords, doing his best to ignore the dog growling from behind the majolica umbrella stand. That was a plum. Worth a couple grand, easily.

The woman—her name had slipped away again—stared at his card. Heavy diamond rings hung from her twisted fingers.

"Mr. Doré, I want to say right now that I'm going to get a second opinion."

"Of course." Women always said this. He dropped his voice half an octave. "It is best to go slowly, after such a loss."

"Sixty-two years."

"I can't imagine . . . "

"And not a day apart."

Wishing she would invite him beyond the foyer, Bernard lowered his gaze and nodded, trying to express sympathy without opening the floodgates to her detailing those sixty-two years. "My purpose is to make this process as simple as possible. After I've looked around—" He waved toward the living room. "In a few days, I'll give you an estimate. You'll find my arrangements superior to anyone else's."

"I'm just saying, I'm going to get a second opinion."

He looked directly at her, about to say that he would do the same in her place, but stopped, unnerved by how her wig had lifted from her temple to reveal a small gap, no more than a quarter of an inch. Picturing her puckered skull, Bernard's heart raced. He squeezed his fist in his pocket and forced his gaze away, toward the living room and concentrated on what he could see. Big brocade couch. Fireplace with a corroded brass fan. Above, on the mantelpiece, a nice bit of Meissen. Yes, very nice. All but lost among the usual brass candlesticks and mid-century wedding photographs. The vise in his chest eased. Exhaling slowly, he calculated what the photographs would be worth as the pain retreated to a cave below his armpit. Scarcely ten dollars a pop, including the crystal frames, if they were crystal. The dog lunged for him.

The woman hissed, "Mr. Rogers, where are your manners?"

Bernard jerked back, trying to get a fix on the blur of her face below the orange wig. Rogers? The blur swayed in his direction and whispered, "I'm going to have to lock you up."

Alarmed, fighting the twinge below his arm, Bernard watched the old woman bend stiffly. She picked up the dog, trotted down the shadowy hall, threw it into the first bedroom, and slammed the door. So the dog was Rogers.

Feeling foolish, Bernard tried to steady his breath. The dog yodeled. The woman waited. Between the yelps and scratching, Bernard heard a sound, very faint, and oddly familiar. A clicking maybe, but not exactly. It vanished, drowned out by the damn dog's yapping. As Bernard strained to catch the sound again—it seemed urgent that he identify whatever it was—stillness settled around him, a bell-like vacuum through which he could just make out the dog's barking, until that faded, and there was only silence. An unaccountable disappointment washed through him. What was going on? He closed his eyes and felt as if he were tumbling through space. He flung out his arm and knocked something hard. He opened his eyes to a seam in the wallpaper, and moved his finger up the edge, the straight line drawing him back onto solid ground.

The woman was now beside him. Her eyes roamed over his face. Without her glasses, her eyes were startling. Her mouth formed words that didn't reach him. Again came plock plauck, plock plauck. He took a handkerchief from his pocket and wiped sweat from above his lip, listening to what he now recognized, the rhythm of a limping man hurrying on a boardwalk. Hurrying to? Or from? He'd always wondered. His heart skipped with pleasure. It was, it had to be, an 1815 Couquard.

Tamping down his excitement, he followed the woman into the living room. A pair of Grand Rapids end tables. Bookcase filled with Japanese porcelains. Two dusty black recliners facing a TV. An ormolu candelabra.

The Couquard clock nowhere in sight. The woman motioned him toward the monstrous brocade couch.

The Couquard Lauron family, based in Bruges and renowned throughout Europe from the late seventeenth through the early nineteenth centuries, built freestanding, wall-mounted, and miniature timepieces that were sought-after symbols of wealth, refinement, and modernity. One hundred years after Galileo's discovery of the pendulum in 1581, the Couquard Lauron firm was among the first to apply this source of regular and reliable power to clocks.

He'd written these words for the fall 1964 Harmon & de Chalbert auction catalogue, forty-plus years ago. Hiding his excitement, he waited for the woman to ease herself onto the other end of the couch, then he sat, too, no longer able to hear the distinctive ticking, yet buoyed by the certainty that somewhere in this dreary apartment the Couquard was waiting for him.

What distinguishes the Couquard Lauron from other fine timepieces of the era are the anchor and escape wheel made of an exceedingly durable metal alloy (formula unknown) and the superlative craftsmanship in all the mechanical works. Additionally, the inventive, rather austere case designs, which typify the Couquard Lauron of the nineteenth century, are much in keeping with our own, late twentieth century tastes and make the rare appearance of a Couquard Lauron on the market a noteworthy event.

With a clarity that often visited Bernard in dreams, Philippe was alive again, bustling with energy, this time striding around the prep room, barking orders. Standing next to an open shipping crate, Philippe slapped his hands together, then lifted out of the excelsior an oblong wall clock, sparkling with mother-of-pearl and gold inlay. "Bernard, it is at moments like this," he said, grinning, his narrow face alight, "when the unexpected happens, in this case an unparalleled treasure coming from an ignorant trust in Oklahoma City, that makes our business so worthwhile."

Something slipped. A light flashed. Philippe disappeared and Bernard was no longer young and lithe, but old and sitting on an ugly couch in a strange living room.

". . . without a lot of people traipsing through." The woman with the wig scowled at him.

Jerked from his dream, Bernard stopped himself from crying out. He cleared his throat and started his spiel about how he would proceed with appraisal and, if she wished, with sales. He could give her only an "estimated range of value," anything else would be unreliable, even "deceptive," his tone implying that, except for him, the appraisal field was rife with the unscrupulous. That she might call in someone else to claim the Couquard sickened him.

"What about the whatall that your fancy collectors won't want?"

He mentioned his picker who'd take everything else and his cleaning service. "Not even dust will be left."

"I like that."

Caroline sat back, staring through the over-eager, now red-faced man and thought about the model apartment at the Mission Hills Retirement Community where Ronald had put down a deposit on a two bedroom "for you and Mr. Rogers, after I'm gone." She didn't want to live in such a place. Beige walls, beige carpet, beige upholstered chairs. She recalled the light from the picture window blotting out the sales brochures that had been fanned out on the dining table, and the image disappeared and she was standing in a hilltop temple outside Kyoto, with sunlight dazzling in from all four sides. She and Ronald were in the center of the pavilion with clumps of other tourists beneath the high wooden ceiling, and Ronald was complaining about his knees. "Those damn switchback stairs," he said, and told her to hold her camera closer. "You don't know who these people are." She turned from him and saw that between the thick red columns the view was blocked by fog. They could be in a cloud. Ronald hissed more instructions.

Annoyed, she turned away and was surprised to see a stranger, the appraiser, and she was in her own living room. Embarrassed, wondering how long her mind had been wandering, she said, "My husband used to take care of all this kind of business."

The man nodded, his thick white hair falling forward. "He would want you to be well taken care of now."

Taken care of, right up to the end, and past. She had her directives for after he was gone: consult with Milt before making any decisions; don't listen to Kay; never take more than the minimum payout. She smacked her hands on her skirt, irked by his orders.

"Mr. Doré, let's see what you've got to say."

Down to business. Bernard imagined the Couquard, not far away. He smoothed his necktie, trying to quiet the slight flutter in his chest, and stood. "Let's begin right here, if that's convenient?"

The ormolu candelabra would bring in three thousand, he told her— more than it was worth, but he'd make it up elsewhere—the Meissen platter, over two thousand. Alas, the bird's eye maple chest, not more than seventy. In truth, it would fetch closer to seven hundred. It was Philippe who'd taught him to careen between high and low to undermine any confidence clients might have in their own judgment. "But always provide lots of highs," Philippe insisted. "Feed the greed." As Bernard reeled off prices for the Japanese porcelains, he could see the quiver of excitement in Mrs. Bledsoe's eyes, and the flash of disappointment at the price he quoted for the brasses. Hope, dismay, and the desire to please, all these impulses he knew how to work. So much he'd learned from Philippe, and how appalled Philippe would be by what Bernard had become, an appraiser to old ladies, not museums, not fine collections. Philippe would have to admit, though, that Bernard was still a pro.

The woman led him to the library, where he could no longer hear even the aftereffect of ticking. Suppressing his eagerness to find the Couquard, he mentioned five thousand for the roll-top desk, eight hundred for the reproduction Tiffany lamp, the books, sadly, had little market value. "You might want to donate them."

"You do it."

She was his.

She led him toward the hall, where he could just make out the Couquard's tick, which was interrupted by its chime: three golden rings. Unmistakable. His heart leapt. The woman paused to open a cupboard filled with shelves of geodes. Geodes. Good god. Bernard waited. The chimes sounded again. He trembled with delight.

Perhaps the finest clock produced in the Couquard Lauron workshop was the eighteen fifteen, eight-day repeater, a clock that strikes the hour and then, three minutes later, strikes again.

Just like Philippe's. Masking his agitation, Bernard praised the worthless stones, lying that he knew a collector who'd be interested. The woman chortled with pleasure.

At last they were walking toward the ticking. There, in the dining room, was the Couquard. Bernard's chest tightened. Weak-kneed, he walked toward the clock. It was a superb specimen, although not quite as fine as Philippe's. Brushing his fingertips over its black, lacquered frame, Bernard reminded himself that Philippe had never actually owned the Couquard; it had only passed through his hands. This one was outstanding: square, not the usual oval, eighteen inches on a side, with a mother-of-pearl inlay surround, and on its face, behind the glass and the ornate hands, a painted seascape. Philippe's had had a forest scene. A brook overarched by two thin pines.

Bernard leaned closer. If Philippe's clock had entered his life, their lives, one year later, even six months later, it might have saved him, in spite of the fake Munchs, the controversy over the Vlaminck, the dust-up over taxes. By then, it had long since been sold, for too little, Philippe complained.

"You can't leave me now," Philippe had said. "You can't work for Albemarle. It's absurd."

Bernard had set his Rolodex in his packing box and said nothing. What was there to say? That Philippe had destroyed Harmon & de Chalbert and would be lucky to avoid jail. That there was nothing left here for Bernard. Philippe grabbed the Rolodex. "Company property, Bernard. You're not taking my clients to Albemarle."

A few months later, Harmon & de Chalbert was in receivership and Philippe was living with his sister in Queens. Bernard was in Zurich evaluating the Hofmeister porcelains when he next spoke to Philippe. It was late, the middle of the night when the hotel phone rang.

"Come back, Bernard. We'll move the business to Miami—"

Even over the spotty trans-Atlantic connection, Bernard could hear the booze. "Philippe, it won't work. You know that. It's a one-way street."

"—and we'll set up as partners."

Bernard stared across his hotel room as impatience, fury, and shame descended. He reminded Philippe that he'd been barred from the auction business, and no museum would touch him. Philippe talked about loose money in Florida, the transplants from New York, the Cuban money, all nonsense.

"Are you there, Bernard?"

"Yes."

"Dear boy, you've got to help me. I am surrounded by grayness and cold. I need sunshine, sunshine every day."

"Philippe, if I find anything special, an unexpected gem, I'll hold it back from Albemarle and send it your way." Which Philippe would know he couldn't risk. It would cost Bernard his job.

The line went silent, then Philippe said, "What kind of a prick are you?"

Bernard hung up. A week later Philippe's cleaning lady found him dead. After the funeral, Philippe's sister sent him the newspaper photograph of the two of them, he and Philippe, at the sale of the Canova Venus, Bernard behind Philippe looking like what he was, a corn-fed kid.

A voice broke in, a woman's. "That clock's been in my family since I was little. Are you all right?"

Bernard struggled to get his bearings. "A lovely timepiece," he managed to whisper.

"Timepiece, that's what my Papa called it, too." Caroline felt sorry for the appraiser. She told him how, when she was a girl, in the fall, after the harvest, Papa would drive the wagon to town, filled with the extras of what Mama had put up from her garden. "Chowchow, pickled water-melon rind, stewed tomatoes, peach butter, the kind of thing folks who moved from the country could no longer produce for themselves but they wanted."

"Chowchow, I haven't heard that word in decades," Mr. Doré said, the white patches on his cheeks beginning to color.

Relieved he wasn't going faint on her, Caroline went on. "I was about six years old when Papa came back from town carrying a big somethin' wrapped in a tatty quilt. Mama asked what it was and Papa said, 'It's the finest timepiece you've ever seen.' He folded back the quilt and there it was, this very clock, sparkling with pearls and gold."

Mama had been angry. She'd shouted that Papa had sold the labor of her hands for this useless thing. Papa pulled from his vest pocket a small metal disc with a long hook and held it before Caroline's face. "This here's the pendulum," he said. Terrified, Caroline hadn't moved, and Mama stalked from the kitchen. Never did Mama speak of the clock, though each Sunday after prayers, she would wind it with a sharp-elbowed, sour intensity that silenced conversation until after luncheon. When Papa died, she hung a towel over it.

Caroline turned to Mr. Doré. "The original key I keep here." She lifted the glass cover. "It's supposed to run for eight days, but I wind it every Sunday."

"These days, most people don't want the trouble of a wind-up clock."

"I can understand that," she said. "My mother gave it to us as a wedding present."

That Mama had given them something that she loathed as a wedding present, no less, had lodged in Caroline's heart like a needle. "Why would Mama do this?" she had cried to Ronald, when the boy delivered it. "Don't you go asking her," he'd said, insisting that Mama had given them a family heirloom.

She turned to the appraiser. "My husband said it must be worth something."

"Something, certainly," Mr. Doré said, as if he doubted it. "Perhaps we might see what else. . ."

"I have a full butler's pantry," she said, worried that she didn't have enough to make this worth his while. Had the clock jinxed yet one more thing?

Mr. Doré settled on the stepstool in the butler's pantry with his notepad and she stared at all the needless stuff she should have gotten rid of years ago: warped cookie tins, gravy boats, seltzer bottles you couldn't get cartridges for any more. Why had she been so avid about Venetian glass? Or footed cake platters? Mama was right about one thing. What you needed was what you used up: sugar, cloth, a sack of oranges. Caroline thought of the Japanese temple. She heard the wind rush beneath its roof. She asked Mr. Doré if he would like a cup of tea. He would.

As soon as she left, Bernard dug out his inhaler. Two puffs. "Hands massaging my lungs, that's what it's like," he'd said to the doctor, who'd insisted on tests. "No tests," Bernard had said. He knew what he needed, not tests and no more procedures. What he needed was a little place on the beach. He gasped as the chill hit, then inhaled tentatively, his chest clearing. He shoved the inhaler into his pocket. With luck, and a few more like this woman, Seaside would be within his reach. He scanned the shelves, cheered by the prospect of what lay ahead, a decent profit on the old lady's goods, and the Couquard, which he would keep. As he contemplated this, deep inside him a lightness uncoiled and he was within that lightness that, had he been required to describe it, he would have said was a sun-shot cavernous stage, but without floor or ceiling or any edges, a place with no concrete physical details, all incandescence. Beside him was Philippe, but neither of them had a physical presence, and in this radiant spaciousness he was giving the Couquard to Philippe, and Philippe was accepting it. This giving and accepting were not gestures that began and ended, but were inclinations, fluid, constant, like water spilling from his cupped hand into Philippe's.

From the kitchen, Caroline watched Mr. Doré reposition himself on the stool. She was tired of having him here, tired of having him look at her things, tired of having to consider so much that no longer mattered. She took down the Japanese teapot, touching her finger to its raised chrysanthemum blossom and was again in the temple outside Kyoto. The crowds were gone, leaving a hush. In the fog beyond the columns, figures in gray and white glided by. Heads shorn, they might be monks. Or nuns. They moved like dancers.

The kettle shrieked. The clock in the dining room chimed the half-hour. She wished she had lived a different life.

"Mrs. Bledsoe?"

The appraiser eyed her from across the kitchen table. How long had he been sitting there? Between them sat the teapot, steam coiling upward from its spout. When had she filled it? Hiding her dismay, she poured tea into his cup, then hers, spilling a trail of drops on his papers. He wiped them away and spoke about auction versus private sale, the pluses and minuses of each.

"I've had enough. Sell everything."

He blinked, a frog blink.

"Everything, and right away," she repeated. He could steal her blind. What did it matter? "As quickly as possible."

He pursed his too-plump lips, and nodded. "It can be arranged." He inched his tea mug into line with the edge of his notepad. "As early as next week, if you like, but you'll want to set aside a few things, clothes, a few—"

"Clothes, too. Sell all of it."

He lifted one hand to smooth his hair, trying to quash a smile just like Ronald's that said she was a silly, weak woman.

"I mean it. My jewelry too. Sell all of it." She struggled to get off her wedding ring, ignoring his protests, her knuckle turning white as she fought with Ronald's mother's diamonds, unable to budge them. Wanting to cry, she slapped the table instead. From the other room Mr. Rogers erupted.

"And sell Mr. Rogers, too."

"Maybe we should take this in stages." The appraiser's cheeks trembled with alarm.

"I can find someone else, if you're not interested."

"There's no need . . . "

She could walk out the door and not come back. She could take Mr. Rogers to the park and let him loose and just keep walking. She would go to Japan, to the Buddhists. They would gather around her, gentle figures in gray and white, heads smooth as river stones, individuality erased, all vanity and acquisitiveness, all pain and yearning gone.

"I'm going to Japan."

"Japan's lovely this time of year." He was patronizing her. She was too tired to care.

"I might stay."

"To get away, I think of that, too."

Surprised, she glanced up and saw that his eyes were closed. "Yes," she said.

His labored breath slowed and grew steady. From a distance came the sound of street traffic. The clock in the dining room chimed, echoing in the silence.

"A very fine clock," the appraiser said.

"Near eighty years in my family."

"Almost half its life."

Did clocks have lives? she wondered, picturing it on the opposite side of the wall behind the appraiser, its face becoming human and full of malice. "I've always hated that clock."

The appraiser nodded, as if he understood. Together they listened to it tick.

Beneath the sound, Caroline heard the dog scuffling. "You must find Mr. Rogers a good home."

"Mrs. Bledsoe, if need be, I'll take your dog myself."

And take him right to an animal shelter, she thought, not particularly caring. A worm-vein in his throat pulsed to the clock's tick while he spoke of a private sale, of packers and movers. She pictured the apartment emptied, her things in a dusty antique shop where a young woman, a blonde in a pretty yellow sun dress, moved among the armoires and stacked tables, her hand grazing tea towels, picking up a bowl, putting it down. She smiled at a jumble of tarnished soupspoons. She comes upon Caroline's clock. Her charm bracelet tinkles as she touches it. The fancy, pearled inlay, the scalloped frame, the wavy glass, all this delights her. This poor girl is so innocent. Caroline shivered.

Years ago, when Ronald had overheard Caroline talking to the clock repairman, he yelled, "You can't sell the clock."

"Why not? Mama's dead," Caroline had protested.

"You cannot sell it, do you hear? It's an heirloom. I forbid it."

After Mama died, when Ronald began to change, Caroline had known that it was the clock's doing. Into her home, too, it had brought evil.

From the archway behind the appraiser, the girl in the yellow dress looked at Caroline. Caroline clenched her fingers, wanting to cry out, to warn her, as the appraiser laid out papers on the table. He pushed a pen toward Caroline, and she knew what she had to do. She pulled off her wig and put it next to her teacup. Her scalp prickled. A light breeze circled her head, like spring. The appraiser stared at her. Around her she could feel others she couldn't see press close: Ronald, her parents, long dead friends, the crossing-guard, neighbors from their first home, so many she'd forgotten, so many she'd loved, and, at the outer edges of the shifting crowd, the Buddhist monks or nuns, hovering like ghosts.

"One thing, Mr. Doré, the clock in the dining room, I don't want it going to someone else. I want you to destroy it."

His face caved in like a sinkhole as he reached for her hands. Caroline was sorry. She didn't want to agitate him. He was, after all, helping her. As she tried to get a fix on him to explain, she realized that he was looking through her, like Ronald.

She pulled her hands from his. "I want you to smash that clock, do you hear?"

His tongue darted out and flicked the corner of his mouth. "Mrs. Bledsoe, I can't do that."

"Then I'll do it myself."

Far away Mr. Rogers began barking. She stood, her knees wobbly, and inched toward the dining room. The appraiser stood, bobbing his head, coaxing her to sit down.

"Get out of my house," she cried, and pushed past him, but her hands missed his chest and she stumbled sideways and slammed her shoulder against the table as she fell. She tried to scream at him, but couldn't. Nor could she move, with one arm pinned beneath her. Crumbs dug into her cheek. She couldn't see or feel her legs. Mr. Rogers barked on and on, and the man tugged at his collar, feet splayed, swaying like a drunk. Such a fool. She watched his face bulge and grow waxy, wanting to tell him that none of this mattered, not the clock or the dog or all the worthless things acquired in a lifetime, but explaining wasn't worth the effort. She was unspeakably tired. Above her the room dimmed, folding in on itself as the man's legs slid out slowly from beneath him until he was sitting against the stove with one stocking foot jammed into her hip. This was oddly comforting. Cold from the floor crept along her cheek and over her scalp. Had Ronald left the front door open? It didn't matter.

Afraid to move, Bernard watched the woman's unwavering eye. Behind him, the clock ticked, like a man, he was now certain, limping away.

Acknowledgements

After watching the Academy Awards, and wishing the excited winners would hustle through their too-long recitations of acknowledgements, I recognize that we are all indebted to far more people than we can ever thank and, in a public setting, short is better than long.

My boundless gratitude goes to:

To the editors who chose my stories for their journals—thank you thank you.

To my dear writing friends who have read these stories through many drafts—I send you bouquets of thanks and wishes for more to come.

To Fred Shafer, teacher and mentor—my thanks don't quit. Your lessons will always guide me.

To the Ragdale Foundation for the time and space to write—thank you.

To Marc Estrin and Donna Bister, the wise and giving souls of Fomite Press—I can't thank you enough.

To my parents, Tom and Caryl Sloan, who gave me the world, and to my children, Andrew and Jane, who enlarged it—every day I give thanks for you.

To my husband and my love, Jeff Rosen, for everything—there are no sufficient words.

Lynn Sloan is a writer and photographer. Her stories have appeared in *Ploughshares, Shenandoah,* and *American Literary Review,* among other publications, and been nominated for the Pushcart Prize. She is the author of the novel *Principles of Navigation* (2015 Fomite). Her fine art photographs have been exhibited nationally and internationally. For many years she taught photography at Columbia College Chicago, where she founded the *journal Occasional Readings in Photography,* and contributed to *Afterimage, Art Week,* and *Exposure.* She lives in Evanston, Illinois with her husband.

About Fomite

A fomite is a medium capable of transmitting infectious organisms from one individual to another.

"The activity of art is based on the capacity of people to be infected by the feelings of others." Tolstoy, *What Is Art?*

Writing a review on Amazon, Good Reads, Shelfari, Library Thing or other social media sites for readers will help the progress of independent publishing. To submit a review, go to the book page on any of the sites and follow the links for reviews. Books from independent presses rely on reader to reader communications.

For more information or to order any of our books, visit
http://www.fomitepress.com/FOMITE/Our_Books.html

More Titles from Fomite...

Novels
Joshua Amses — *During This, Our Nadir*
Joshua Amses — *Raven or Crow*
Joshua Amses — *The Moment Before an Injury*
Jaysinh Birjepatel — *The Good Muslim of Jackson Heights*
Jaysinh Birjepatel — *Nothing Beside Remains*
David Brizer — *Victor Rand*
Dan Chodorkoff — *Loisaida*
David Cleveland — *Time's Betrayal*
Paula Closson Buck — *Summer on the Cold War Planet*
David Adams Cleveland — *Time's Betrayal*
Jaimee Wriston Colbert — *Vanishing Acts*
Roger Coleman — *Skywreck Afternoons*
Marc Estrin — *Hyde*
Marc Estrin — *Kafka's Roach*
Marc Estrin — *Speckled Vanities*

Fomite

Fomite

Tom Walker — *Signed Confessions*
Silas Dent Zobal — *The Inconvenience of the Wings*

Odd Birds

Micheal Breiner — *the way none of this happened*
J. C. Ellefson — *Under the Influence*
David Ross Gunn — *Cautionary Chronicles*
Andrei Guriuanu — *The Darkest City*
Gail Holst-Warhaft — *The Fall of Athens*
Roger Leboitz — *A Guide to the Western Slopes and the Outlying Area*
dug Nap— *Artsy Fartsy*
Delia Bell Robinson — *A Shirtwaist Story*
Peter Schumann — *Bread & Sentences*
Peter Schumann — *Charlotte Salomon*
Peter Schumann — *Faust 3*
Peter Schumann — *Planet Kasper, Volumes One and Two*
Peter Schumann — *We*

Plays

Stephen Goldberg — *Screwed and Other Plays*
Michele Markarian — *Unborn Children of America*

18206243R00136

Made in the USA
Lexington, KY
21 November 2018